
★

A sudden roar, as loud as an aircraft engine, blasted from somewhere behind. Lilli turned and saw an airboat zooming over the water like a hydroplane. It barreled toward them. She caught a glimpse of the driver, wearing a wet suit and goggles. Terror gripped Lilli. She screamed, hoping against all hope that the driver would turn away in time. She prayed that she and Zack would survive.

The airboat bounced hard on the water. Wave after wave battered the tiny canoe. Lilli's life jacket flew from her lap. Her paddle fell into the water. The canoe rocked side to side, and then flipped over. Down, down Lilli sank into the murky waters, her boots as heavy as cement shoes. Fear turned to panic. She couldn't see. Her lungs felt as if they would burst. Sputtering, gulping air, Lilli finally broke through the surface.

★

Previously published Worldwide Mystery titles by
DIANE SAWYER

THE MONTAUK MYSTERY
THE MONTAUK STEPS

Diane Sawyer

the TOMOKA MYSTERY

W🌐RLDWIDE®

TORONTO • NEW YORK • LONDON
AMSTERDAM • PARIS • SYDNEY • HAMBURG
STOCKHOLM • ATHENS • TOKYO • MILAN
MADRID • WARSAW • BUDAPEST • AUCKLAND

To my husband, Robert,
for his love and understanding.

Recycling programs
for this product may
not exist in your area.

THE TOMOKA MYSTERY

A Worldwide Mystery/April 2011

First published by Avalon Books

ISBN-13: 978-0-373-26750-7

Printed in U.S.A.

Acknowledgments

To Kirk and Linda Sawyer, and to Barrie and Luis Buenaventura, for their encouragement, love and enthusiasm.

To Colin Sawyer, Cael Sawyer and Sonia Buenaventura for their unconditional love and wisdom beyond their years.

To Grace Murdock and Peggy Nolan, gracious and talented St. Petersburg writers and exceptional friends, for their advice and continued interest in my work.

To Marjorie Jackson, writer and dear friend, for her helpful comments and counsel.

To those family members and friends who encouraged me, especially Linda Prince, my Monday-morning "walk and talk" confidante.

To Sue DeLong, Recreation Center Supervisor, for inviting me to join the Up and Down Tennis League, and the formidable players who demonstrated courage as well as skill.

To Joe Isaacs, Park Services Specialist at the Tomoka Basin GEOpark for sharing information, explaining artifacts and making the history of the area come to life.

To good friends Marcella and Jim Barnes, who opened their hearts and home while I researched Tomoka Park and the surrounding communities.

And last but not least, to Erin Cartwright, Senior Editor at Avalon Books, for her insightful suggestions, which honed the characters and clarified the plot.

ONE

Emergency Girlfriend

LILLI MASTERS SAT AT HER rolltop desk, staring at her computer's swirling screen saver. She couldn't bring herself to finish the "Wild and Wacky Weddings" article for *Viewpoint* magazine. Photographs of skydiving brides and grooms, happy couples perched in air-balloon baskets, not to mention an entire wedding party wearing gorilla costumes, needed captions and text. They would have to wait. Her love life—every disappointing and discouraging moment of it—consumed her thoughts.

Leaning back in her desk chair, Lilli rattled the ice cubes in her raspberry tea and rubbed the cool glass against her forehead. She wasn't being unrealistic or unreasonable. Absolutely not! She didn't expect her chance meeting with a handsome detective at the end of the summer to blossom into a torrid autumn romance. But was an occasional email, fax or telegram too much to ask? Smoke signals, anything would do! After Zack's two brief but welcome phone calls…nothing. Four weeks of nothing, to be exact. Was he bored with her? Had she uttered an unexpected faux pas? Or was it simply the old bugaboo of men and their inexplicable communications skills?

Lilli had met Zack Faraday during Labor Day weekend in Grayrocks, a resort town on the eastern tip of Long Island, New York. She went to the Baywatch Inn to photograph the holiday festivities for *Viewpoint* magazine. Zack, a New York City detective, was in town to attend his cousin's wedding. Their paths crossed in a popular tourist spot, and they hit it off immediately. Over lunch, Lilli mentioned that while photographing the quaint town, she intended to look for two women who were missing from the Baywatch Inn. Zack's detective instincts kicked in. He offered to help. They spent many pleasant hours questioning the townsfolk and exploring the area.

Sparks heated up. During the weekend, Lilli and Zack "kindled the flames of infatuation"—that's what her best friend Sue called "getting to know each other." Lilli had never met anyone like Zack—so sexy, so amusing, so… just thinking about him made her weak in the knees. Sure, he had his faults. He shied away from commitment, was unwilling to reveal his feelings, and put work above romance. But after all, Zack was a man. Those imperfections came with the territory.

Their romance was interrupted when a mysterious stranger stole Lilli's camera, destroyed her work and threatened her life. The local police were called in. They tied Lilli's assailant to the missing women. A manhunt began. Things spiraled out of control and Lilli barely survived several harrowing experiences. Zack became her hero, her knight in shining armor. He risked everything to save her and bring a murderer to justice.

She had expected to see him again. But summer had faded. Pumpkins now lined the roadside stands near her cottage in Suffern, a tiny village one hour north of New York City, and the relationship was going nowhere. The two times Zack had telephoned, he postponed getting together, saying he was tied up with a big case, and would she take a rain check on the romantic evening they had planned. For gosh sakes, why couldn't Zack be like the detectives in movies and TV shows? They captured lots of bad guys, but they still found time to romance their sweethearts.

Lilli peered out the window at the towering blue spruces shading her front lawn. Weeds were overtaking the beds of chrysanthemums and the wood-chip path leading to her front door. Her mind floated back to three years ago, when she had stopped to buy gas in Suffern. Glancing up a side street, she'd noticed a hand-painted For Rent sign tacked to a mailbox fashioned from a well pump. She had immediately fallen in love with the tiny fieldstone cottage. How could she resist the porch swing, weathered oak door, oversized chimney and ivy-covered garden wall? Giving no thought to heating bills, weeding, raking or snow shoveling, she had signed the lease, given up her seventh-floor studio walk-up in the Bronx and, over the protests of her friends, moved in.

The meager possessions she had collected since

graduating from Fordham University six years earlier barely filled her Bronco. No problem! She furnished the cottage with treasures from local garage sales and church bazaars. Her first purchase, a matching over-stuffed couch, chair and ottoman in tweedy greens and browns, determined her woodsy decor. When her friend Sue saw the cottage for the first time, she said, "It looks like the kind of place where lusty Maid Marion would lure Robin Hood."

Well, Robin Hood hadn't appeared. And neither had Zack Faraday.

Lilli swallowed the last gulp of tea and promised herself to get to the weeding by noon. Then she'd hike into the Ramapo Mountains for kindling wood to feed her cavernous fireplace. Planning ahead, she had slipped into her worn grass-stained jeans and ripped flannel shirt, which she planned to toss in the trash when she'd finished her chores. But first she would allow herself the luxury of rereading the email from her brother, Pete, an adventure guide, who, last she knew, was enjoying a pisco sour at the Internet Café in Cuzco, Peru.

"Lilli: Come on down and join my group. We're going to climb Machu Picchu, fly over the Nazca Lines and— you can't resist this—photograph the butterflies at Lake Sandoval. What's the point of being a freelance photo-journalist if you can't travel to exotic places whenever you want? Say yes. I'll call soon. Love, Pete."

R-r-r-r-ring! The phone's blaring peal startled

Lilli. Pete was impulsive, but that couldn't be him. Not that fast.

"Lilli?" Her heart skipped a beat at the sound of Zack Faraday's husky voice. "How are you?"

"Does this call have anything to do with a rain check?" Why waste time? Come straight to the point before his work called him away, like the last two times.

Zack laughed. She could pictured his ruggedly hand- some face, the mesmerizing eyes, the crooked grin, the scar on his chin that made people look twice, wondering if he were Harrison Ford.

"Lilli, I need a favor."

"So this isn't about a date."

"An emergency has come up. I need a girlfriend for a few days."

"And you immediately thought of me."

"Of course. You were number one on my short list."

"Would you care to elaborate?"

"Sure. You're fun. You have a sense of adventure—"

"I meant exactly how many names are on your list?"

"You sound annoyed, Lilli. Uh, this isn't going as well as I'd expected. Any chance we could continue this face-to-face?"

"Like when?"

"How about right now?"

"Where are you?"

"At your back door."

Lilli jumped to her feet, darted into the hallway and glanced at her reflection in the antique crackled mirror. No makeup. Big owlish glasses monopolized her face while her contact lenses soaked. Unruly curls sprang from her ponytail. She looked like a red-headed Medusa in rags! "What are you doing out there?"

"I'm standing between mounds of mulch and bags of dehydrated cow manure, wondering how to convince you to leave all this behind and come away with me to Florida."

Lilli flung open the door and growled, "You could have given me some notice instead of tracking me down like one of your fugitives." Her glasses slipped down below the bridge of her nose.

Zack turned off his cell phone and handed her a gift bag with tissue paper poking out of the top. "You look great! Even better than I remembered."

"How nice to see you…at last," she said, stepping aside to let him enter. The slamming door nearly caught the backs of his loafers. He looked like he'd come from a *Gentleman's Quarterly* photo shoot. Olive green slacks, black windbreaker, shirt with flecks of olive green, black and brown. "Nice clothes. Are you trying to impress me?"

"Heck no, it's my sister I want to impress. Every time I see her, she says, 'You look haggard.' That's her favorite word. 'Haggard.' Then she disappears into her kitchen and starts whipping up soybean shakes and herbal hors d'oeuvres. 'Try these,' she says, cornering me and cackling like a witch offering a brew of toads and slugs. 'You'll feel better and look better in no time.'"

"What's your sister got to do with this?"

"I…we, you and me, we're going to her condo in Orlando Beach, Florida, for a few days." He checked his watch. "She's expecting us for dinner. She can't wait to meet you."

"You'd better tell me what this Florida trip is all about. And I can't wait to hear about this emergency girlfriend idea." Lilli marched toward the fireplace and plunked down on the edge of the ottoman.

Zack eased his lanky body into a chair. "I've sure missed you," he said and his gaze made Lilli feel warm all over. "I've wanted to see you for weeks, but for security reasons I couldn't give away my whereabouts. Besides, the case I was on was…messy…the kind of mess that gets a relationship off to a bad start. I wanted to wait until it was over."

"You look haggard," Lilli said, noticing the dark circles under his eyes.

"Geez, I hope you're not planning to whip up a carrot cocktail or seaweed shake."

"Maybe a toad burger."

They both laughed. "How about a glass of raspberry tea?" she said.

"Sounds good." He followed her into the brick-floored galley kitchen and leaned back against the sink. She opened the refrigerator, took out the pitcher of tea, and reached past Zack for the sugar bowl. He put his arm around her waist and drew her close. "I've been thinking about this moment for a long time," he said and kissed her on the lips. She set the pitcher down and put her arms around his neck, surrendering to his considerable charm. "I've been thinking about this moment, too."

Their kisses became longer, more passionate. Lilli's heart galloped. Sexy images of Zack and her flashed through her mind, images she had been dreaming about since they'd first met. Held in his strong embrace, Lilli almost forgot that Zack had ignored her for weeks. Then she snapped to her senses. Zack had some nerve! He thought he could come back into her life and she would drop everything and race off to Florida with him. Well, he'd better think again! She had a career, friends, obligations. Closets to clean. Tires to rotate.

Zack's right hand cradled the back of Lilli's head and he kissed her on the cheek. His warm breath tickled her ear. "Say you'll come with me to Florida."

Lilli wanted to tell Zack she didn't like being taken for granted, but the words wouldn't form. Had her brain turned to mush?

Zack wrapped his arms tightly around Lilli. She looked up at him. His gray-blue eyes pleaded with her. At that moment, Lilli knew she would go to the ends of the world with Zack Faraday. But she had waited months for him to call, now he could wait for her answer. All was fair in love and…"Why don't you fill in the details," she said, pulling away reluctantly and carrying the glasses back to the living room.

Florida, she thought. Shuffleboard and plastic flamingos. Why couldn't he choose a romantic and exciting place, like Grayrocks, where they'd met? On second thought, she didn't need the excitement of running from a bloodthirsty maniac…but she would welcome a cozy inn, intimate dinner and moonlit stroll along the beach.

Zack clicked the rim of his glass against hers and sat next to her on the ottoman. "The details of the case are gory. There's a dead man in New York City…and a possible connection to a murderous rampage in Florida that took place between Ormond Beach and Daytona Beach. Maybe you remember reading about Benjamin Voda."

"You mean the monster who killed several cops and some innocent bystanders?"

"Yeah. In cold blood. He botched a Seven-Eleven holdup, murdered the store clerk and led the police on a wild chase, killing four innocent bystanders as well as two state troopers and a rookie police officer. They didn't stand a chance. They were up against a career criminal, armed to the teeth, released from prison because of overcrowded conditions. When the SWAT team closed in on the gas station where he'd holed up, Voda shot himself in the head, rather than surrender. Lucky bastard got off too easy killing himself."

"It was in the newspapers for weeks, just before we met," Lilli said, remembering the shattered lives of so many families, the community's numbing grief. And then came heartbreaking pictures of funerals. Grim-faced cops, many of them openly shedding tears, their shields banded in black, saying farewell to their own.

Lilli rubbed her hands briskly over her arms as if to fight off a blast of chilly air. "The only solace is that Voda's dead and he can't harm anyone else."

"That might not be exactly true," Zack said.

"What do you mean?"

"It wasn't released to the public, but later, when Voda's apartment was searched, detectives found an arsenal of semi-automatic rifles, several from countries that deal in drugs, sex slaves and exotic sleaze. He had a record a mile long—burglary, assault, drug possession, and so on—but running illegal guns was his specialty."

Lilli saw the concern etched on Zack's face. "I don't know how you can stand dealing with such hard-core criminals."

"There were outstanding warrants for Voda's arrest in several states, including New York, but I never had the pleasure of meeting him. Before I say more about Voda…or us…let me bring you up to speed on the New York murder."

"Okay," she said begrudgingly, preferring to hear about romance, not crime.

"The body of a well-dressed man was found in an alley in my precinct a few days ago. It looked like a routine mugging death. The wallet was gone, there was no watch or other jewelry. He had been slammed on the back of the head, and bled to death. He didn't match up with any missing persons, the fingerprints turned up nothing and no one claimed the body."

"A mystery man."

"Right. But in going through his clothes, the morgue people found part of a ticket stub in his pocket. Three letters could be made out. O-K-A. Sand particles in his shoes, a certain type of pollen dust, strong traces of indigo dye and other clues placed the man in Florida shortly before his death. The crew went to work sifting through tons of information about tourist attractions and tickets. Bingo! Tomoka State Park in Ormond Beach, Florida, came up the winner. The park was once the stomping grounds of the Timucua Indians who used indigo dye. And the park is very near the places where Benjamin Voda killed his victims."

"That's quite a coincidence," Lilli commented.

Zack nodded. "My boss thinks Voda might have been supplying guns to local criminals. So do I. And the statistics back us up. Florida crimes involving assault weapons went sky-high while Voda was in the area. And now, months after his death, the numbers are still rising. We think someone who knew Voda might have taken over his business. I'm looking for proof and Tomoka Park is where I expect to find it."

Zack leaned forward, his eyes glistening. "Aren't you forgetting something?" He nodded toward the gift he'd brought.

Glad to forget about Voda for a while, Lilli picked

up the bag and pulled away the tissue. Buried beneath a bottle of sunscreen and a sun visor with pink flamingos marching across the brim, she found a dozen rolls of film. "Thanks," Lilli said, touched by Zack's thoughtfulness. "I see you remembered the special brand of film I like for my favorite camera."

He smiled. "Detectives are observant, on duty and off. Like those sexy glasses you're wearing. They're new, aren't they?"

Lilli had forgotten about the unflattering glasses. She yanked them off and set them on the table. "I'm curious," she said, ignoring his question. "Just how does my girlfriend-role play in to all this?"

Zack toyed with Lilli's glasses. "We have a real PR situation on our hands. The people in Ormond Beach haven't recovered from their anger or grief or the constant media attention. My boss wants me to go down there and quietly poke around without stepping on any toes and without arousing suspicion. 'Go with a girlfriend,' he says. 'Act like you're enjoying yourself, not snooping around for evidence.' He wants me to look like a typical tourist, not a detective."

"So by inviting me, you're following orders."

"It's not like that," Zack said. "It's a chance for us to spend time together. If something turns up, I'll check in with the Ormond Beach Police Department and identify myself. It not…" Zack grinned. "I'll force myself to enjoy a vacation with you."

"Gee, thanks. I'll try to make it worth your while,"

Lilli said, her voice dripping with sarcasm. "I'm wondering why your boss chose you. Is it because your sister lives in Ormond Beach and you know the area?"

"There's more to it than that."

Lilli cocked her head. "Like what?"

"There's a personal problem at work. But if you don't mind, I'd rather not talk about it. Another time maybe." Lilli saw the pain in his eyes, the controlled anger in his clenched jaw. Zack continued, "So, to avoid suspicion, we'll go to Tomoka State Park, poke around the Indian sites, and pretend to be a happy couple. Shall I take your smile as a 'yes'?"

"Consider it a 'possible maybe.' I had a better offer earlier this morning."

Zack's shoulders slumped. "You're kidding, right?"

"My brother Pete wants me to meet him in Peru and photograph butterflies."

"That's tough competition," Zack said. "But I can top it. My ace in the hole—motorcycles."

Lilli raised an eyebrow.

"It's Bike Week in Daytona. Thousands of bikers having a wild time. Thousands of motorcycles tearing up the roads. For the first time, Daytona is having an extra bike week, besides the usual one in March, in hopes of bringing in big tourist bucks. Think of the photo opportunities. Lucky for us we can stay with my sister. There won't be a vacant hotel room for miles."

Lilli turned her palms to the ceiling. She lifted one and then the other as if she were weighing two equal packages. "Butterflies in Peru with Pete…Bikers in Florida with Zack. Hmmm, that's a tough call, but—"

"The envelope please. And the winner is—"

"Vroooom! Vroooom!"

TWO

The Trails

ZACK AND LILLI PULLED AWAY from Daytona Beach
International Airport in their rented silver Taurus and
headed toward Kate's condo. What a trip! The roads
swarmed with big shiny motorcycles and bikers, single
and double riders, wearing leather and denim. Lilli had
never seen so many bandanas, tattoos, reflector sunglasses and American flag patches.

There were men and women bikers, pairs of motorcycles in small groups, a dozen Harley Electra-Glide
Classics in single file and entire parades of motorcycles playing follow the leader, weaving from one lane
to the other. Motorcycles were parked at gas stations
and fast-food joints. Handpainted banners announcing
Welcome Bikers and Nonstop Bands waved in front of
bars. Port-o-lets with flashing lights ringed the parking lots like video games with strobe effects in an
arcade. Beer trucks waited while their drivers unloaded
cargo.

Lilli's ears were ringing from the sound of roaring,
sputtering engines and flying gravel. She shot only one
roll of film, and didn't ask Zack to stop to talk to bikers.

She didn't want to arrive late and make a poor impression on Zack's sister. There would be time for photographs tomorrow. She looked forward to photographing the bikers' zest for life and quest for adventure, but she needed an unusual slant. She didn't want the typical muscle-bound men bonding with seductive machines that lured them onto the open road. And doctors, lawyers and accountants who shed their button-down lives for one week of eardrum-splitting exhilaration was an overworked theme. There was even an acronym—RUB— meaning "rich urban biker".

"There's The Trails, Kate's condominium complex." Zack braked and turned onto Saddle Creek Road. He'd been drumming his fingers on the steering wheel and fidgeting with the radio during the ten-mile drive from the airport. Lilli figured he was nervous about her meeting Kate. Kate was the eldest and Zack the youngest in their family. Kate's approval, or disapproval, mattered to him. Or was his nervousness connected to that work-related personal problem he had hinted at? Several times during their flight she had caught him deep in thought, oblivious to her presence beside him. His foreboding expression led her to believe that he was struggling with inner demons.

"What a quiet little corner of paradise," Lilli said as the road meandered past beds of yucca plants, split-leaf rhododendron and exotic flowers. She glimpsed two-story cream-hued stucco buildings with cocoa-brown trim nestled beneath slash pines. To the rear, thick shrubbery and a dense cropping of trees created a natural barrier between the community and surrounding highways. Lilli liked the privacy and relaxed atmosphere. Thank heavens it wasn't one of those gated communities where uniformed guards recorded visitors' license plates and surveillance cameras monitored the grounds waiting for suspicious activity.

Lilli settled back and took in the serenity. The only sounds now were the chirping of birds and the chugging of sprinkler heads as they swirled water into the afternoon sunshine. There was no traffic, except for a dark blue sedan several cross-streets behind them.

"Maybe I'm overreacting," Lilli said, glancing at the side mirror, "but that looks like a gangster's car following us."

"Let's see what they do." Zack took a sharp right. The blue sedan turned left and disappeared around the bend.

"Sorry," Lilli said, feeling foolish.

"It probably belongs to one of the older residents," Zack said. "They like to drive around in cars the size of yachts and dock them in front of their garages. Then they complain that seagulls dive down and try to steal the fresh fish they just bought at the market. That's Florida!"

Lilli laughed at what she assumed was an old joke. She looked beyond the lacy vines that clung to the buildings. "There are screened porches everywhere sprouting like weeds," she remarked.

"I should warn you that Floridians are a rare breed who speak their own language. They call a porch a 'lanai.' Some are screened, some glassed in. Wait until you see Kate's pride and joy." He slowed down as several groups of adults and children rounded the bend, all with towels draped over their shoulders. "You can tell we're getting close to the swimming pool."

Lilli made a big deal of rubbing her eyes when she saw their vibrant bathing suits and cover-ups. "Wow! I've never seen so many tropical prints." She looked from her cinnamon-colored T-shirt, khaki slacks and brown sandals to Zack's dark clothes that he'd worn when he'd arrived at her cottage. "We're going to stand out here," she said.

He smiled. "You'd stand out in any crowd, anywhere."

Before Lilli could say 'thank you,' he added, "All that curly red hair is a real eye-stopper!"

Lilli sighed. Zack sure had a way with compliments.

"They have an Olympic-size pool," Zack said. "Heated to eighty-six degrees, near-freezing to Floridians."

Lilli looked forward to swimming. Not that she had a voluptuous body to pour into her new jade-green spandex one-piece, but it was better than the stretched-out black tank suit she usually wore in underwater layouts. She had packed that along with her goggles and flippers, hoping to do some serious swimming when Zack wasn't around.

"There's Horseshoe Trail," Lilli said, pointing past a cluster of mailboxes shaded by a clump of slash pines. "Didn't you say that was Kate's street?"

"Yes," Zack said and continued past the turn. "But only a direct hit from a hurricane would keep Kate from her Friday afternoon mixed-doubles game." He nodded toward the tennis courts coming up on the left. "There's Kate." He honked, swerved into the parking lot, and pulled to a stop.

Startled, Lilli blinked hard and tried not to stare. A man on one team and a woman on the other team zoomed around the court in wheelchairs, swinging their rackets with one hand while propelling their chairs with the other. Their partners lunged and leaped and ran down balls under their own steam.

"We'll be done soon," the pretty brunette in a pink tennis dress called out cheerily as she steadied her wheelchair. She plucked a tennis ball stuffed in the spokes, tossed it in the air, and blasted it across the net.

"Is that Kate?" Lilli asked, watching the serve kick up shoulder-high.

Zack nodded. "Her opponent, the able-bodied woman, is her closest friend, Betty. She owns a pet store in town. Kate's partner is Oliver, a retired golf pro. Betty's partner, the guy in the chair, is Ike, a financial planner. They've been playing in the same Up-Down league for years."

"Up, you're standing," Lilli guessed. "Down, you're sitting in a chair."

Zack nodded. "The only concession the players in chairs get is two bounces, and the second can be out of bounds. So lots of the action for the players in chairs takes place near the fence and neighboring court. That means the able-bodied players are left to defend much of the court while their partners scramble."

"Watch out!" Lilli exclaimed as Kate charged into the fence to run down a point.

"Don't worry," Zack said. "They're used to the work-out of propelling a twenty-two-pound chair."

"Aren't the side wheels extra large?" Lilli asked.

"Yes, for stability," Zack said. "And see how it's out-fitted with inline skating wheels in the front? That's for quick turns."

"You never mentioned that Kate—" began Lilli.

"I didn't want you to arrive with preconceived no-tions. Kate's strong, stronger than we ever could've imagined."

"What happened to her?" Lilli asked as she stepped out of the car.

"Great backhand, Kate," Zack called out as he guided Lilli toward a shady bench. "It was twelve year ago, June twenty-fifth to be exact. Kate was a successful art-ists' agent then. She had come home for the weekend to celebrate our parents' anniversary and my high school graduation. Tempers flared over some stupid thing and Kate said she needed some fresh air. She went jogging just a half-mile from home, when she heard a truck honking behind her. She moved onto the shoulder. My father, brother and I were pitching horseshoes in our backyard when we heard squealing brakes. My sister Frannie and mother ran outside—"

Zack cleared his throat. "The driver told us that he saw Kate and honked his horn. A rock bounced up and hit his windshield. He was startled and lost control for a second, just one split second, and he veered to the right and clipped Kate. She flew sky-high and landed in a cornfield. We knew the minute we found her lying there that her back was broken. It's been a long road for Kate. Hospitals. Therapy. Rehabilitation. Her personality changed. She can be abrasive and confrontational. But it's understandable, after what she's been through."

Out of the corner of her eye, Lilli saw that same dark blue sedan driving slowly up the next street. She didn't say anything this time. She didn't want Zack to think she was paranoid, but she wondered if someone was spying on them. A detective, Zack was certainly observant, yet he hadn't seemed suspicious of the car or even aware of its presence. Was she overreacting? Or was Zack so glad to see Kate that he was blind to everything else around him?

Zack applauded Kate's forehand volley that won the point after several heated rallies. "Kate moved to Florida—no hills and easy outdoor living. She wanted to make a new life for herself, and she has. Our parents still haven't gotten over the accident. To this day, they blame themselves for insisting she come home and then arguing with her about…well, that's not important. They break down, every time they see her. Kate knows it. She pretends it's Mom's allergies kicking up and offers her Visine. Mom joins in the pretense and accepts it, saying it must be the pollen."

Lilli squeezed Zack's hand. "And all this time I thought you were the brave one in your family."

Zack pushed his sunglasses onto the bridge of his nose. "Kate has me beat by a mile."

In the brief time she had known Zack, he had said little about his family or himself. Yet now he felt free to speak from the heart. Could his confiding in her mean that their brief end-of-summer romance might blossom? No, something else was going on, but she didn't know what.

Lilli tried to concentrate on the tennis game, but she couldn't stop wondering if Zack blamed himself for his sister's accident. His graduation had contributed to Kate's decision to come home. Possibly he'd played a part in the family argument that sent Kate jogging down that road. Lilli felt she was being foolish. Zack wasn't an introspective guy. He probably blamed fate for the truck's collision with Kate.

Lilli shook her head and focused on the game, which was nearing the end of a grueling third-set tie-breaker. Betty and Oliver, the able-bodied players, showed no mercy and Kate and Ike responded with every weapon in their arsenal of shots. Lilli could see that Kate and Ike's legs had atrophied, but their shoulders and arms rippled with muscles. Their upper-body strength amazed her as they wheeled around hitting forehands, backhands, volleys and drop shots.

Avoiding the net and the opponent's overhead shot, Kate and Ike dominated the game from behind the baseline. If a drop shot brought them to the net, they took advantage of the chair's maneuverability and the restraining belt around their chests. Lilli held her breath as Kate spun her chair a one-eighty and raced to the baseline, looking back over her shoulder to track the ball. Lilli exhaled and then applauded as Kate whipped the ball across the net with visible topspin, sinking it into the back corner for the winning point.

"Game, set, match," Oliver exclaimed.

Zack and Lilli applauded as the foursome shook hands and came toward them, wiping their faces on towels and gulping bottled water. Zack ruffled Kate's hair and kissed her cheek. They shared the same profile and good looks.

"Surprise!" Zack said, handing Kate a can of tennis balls with a pink bow on top.

Kate scrutinized the can from every angle.

"What's wrong?" Zack asked.

"Just making sure there are no strings attached," she said.

"Don't start," Zack snapped.

"Meaning I should be sweet and pretend I'm the perfect sister, part of the perfect Faraday family."

"Cut it out," Zack said.

"Fine," Kate growled.

Lilli sensed the tense interaction was over…for the time being. Kate's tennis friends showed no signs of uneasiness. Apparently they were accustomed to the Faraday style of greeting.

"Everyone, this is Lilli Masters," Zack said, all smiles and obviously happy to change the subject. Introductions followed quickly and Lilli complimented everyone on their game. They responded enthusiastically with comments about their individual game and the Up-Down league. Lilli sensed the camaraderie and competitiveness that brought them back week after week for another chance to prove themselves.

Kate gripped Lilli's hand and shook it firmly. "Sorry if I was a bit rough on Zack a minute ago. But he's used to it. We've been practicing for years." She smiled. "In one of our long, friendly conversations—a rare occasion, I might add—Zack told me plenty about you. From what I can see, everything he said is true." She winked and then peered up at Lilli's mane of corkscrew curls, frizzed by the Florida humidity. "And I was sure he was exaggerating."

Ike tapped the wheels of his chair. "I'm off. There's still time to see Disney World and then swim in the ocean before calling it a day."

Everyone laughed.

"It's a joke, Lilli," Kate said. "Tourists' concept of Floridians is spending all day at Disney or the beach.

They don't realize we must work, shop and run errands like ordinary people."

Ike teased, "The Floridian scenario is a fun-filled day followed by an 'early-bird' dinner special. The way they tell it, the early bird is our state bird."

"Here's the best part." Betty juggled two balls and then dropped them in the can. "After the early bird, we come home and sit around sipping margaritas and listening to Jimmy Buffett." Betty zipped her tennis bag.

"Don't forget we plant plastic flamingos and whirli-gigs on our front lawns," Oliver added. Lilli was glad she hadn't worn Zack's gift, the flamingo visor.

Lilli enjoyed the bantering about Florida stereotypes and she jumped right in. "What do you think of the annual winter invasion?" she asked, peering over the frames of her sunglasses. "I hear they're called 'snow birds'? The northerners who spend the entire winter here," she added to be sure she differentiated them from vacationing tourists.

The four stopped in their tracks. Oliver clutched at his chest as if he were having a heart attack. "They fuel our economy, that's the good news." Laugh lines crinkled his weather-bitten face.

"And the bad news?" Lilli asked, squinting into the sun.

"Snowbirds insist on telling us how much better and faster things are done up north. The produce man at the flea market has a sign over his cash register." Oliver chuckled. "'Five-dollar surcharge if you tell me how they pick, weigh or bag fruits and vegetables up north.'"

"Have your fun," Lilli said playfully, "but I detect your New York and New Jersey accents."

"Guilty!" Betty exclaimed. "Noo Yawk born and bred!"

"Got me!" Ike exclaimed. "Noo Joyzey!"

"At least we're not half-backs," Kate added.

Lilli's eyebrows shot up and Kate explained, "People from up north who retire to Florida and then run to the North Carolina mountains for three months to escape the summer heat. Halfway back. Half-backs."

"I'm surprised," Lilli teased. "I thought your blood thinned once you moved to Florida and the heat didn't bother you."

Kate guffawed and then jabbed her brother with the tip of her tennis racket. "Hey, Zack, you look haggard. Come on, I have a new drink that will fix you up."

Zack rolled his eyes and Lilli smothered a laugh.

"See you next week," Ike said and everyone headed to their cars.

"Nice meeting you, Lilli," they called out.

"Same here," she replied.

Oliver tossed his tennis bag in the back seat. "Zack, any chance we can play a round of golf while you're here?"

"Maybe next time," Zack said.

"Looks like you've found better things to do," Oliver replied and Lilli felt herself blush.

As Zack backed out of the parking lot, Lilli saw that Kate had transferred herself from her tennis wheelchair into her street wheelchair and stored the tennis wheelchair in the back of the van. Lilli watched Kate steer herself toward the van. She could only imagine how Kate hoisted herself into her van, reached down, picked up her wheelchair, collapsed it, swung it across her body and set it next to her. Brave woman, Lilli thought, and she promised herself to never complain again about life's little annoyances.

Zack pulled onto Horseshoe Drive.

"Zack, there's that blue sedan again," Lilli said. "It's cruising past where we just turned off. And I saw it when we were watching Kate's tennis match, too."

"The driver has some explaining to do," Zack said. He quickly U-turned and tried to catch up to the car, but it shot ahead. A group of swimmers jumped out of the car's way. Zack jammed down the brake pedal and screeched to a halt. "I'm not going to risk killing someone," he said and turned back to Horseshoe Drive. "But if they show up again, I'll get the plate number and run it. We'll find out who owns it."

Lilli looked at The Trails with wary eyes. An uneasy feeling gnawed at her stomach. Something was about to happen. Something that would shatter the serenity that had lured residents and visitors alike with promises of relaxation and carefree living.

THREE

Kate's Place

ZACK TURNED INTO THE SECOND driveway on the cul-de-sac and parked in front of the garage. "I have my own key," he said, hopping out of the Taurus. "Kate will be along in a minute." He opened the trunk of the car and pulled out their suitcases. "I warned you she can be abrasive, but I hope you'll give her a chance. Underneath that tough exterior, she's still the sweet girl I grew up with."

"Stop apologizing for her," Lilli said. "I'm looking forward to spending time with her."

Juggling her tote bag, which bulged with cameras, notebooks, a tape recorder and a bottle of wine for Kate, Lilli followed Zack along the curving sidewalk to the entry. As soon as the door opened, she felt transported into a breathtaking world of contrasts, of warm rosy pinks and cool sophisticated blacks against stark white walls beneath high vaulted ceilings.

"It's like seeing the world through rose-colored glasses," Lilli exclaimed, taking in the rose carpets, white couches with rose and pink floral designs, black lacquered curio cabinet and tables, and white wicker baskets brimming with pink carnations. Glass and brass glistened throughout the combination dining room and living room that focused on the fireplace and brass-trimmed mirror on the far wall.

Lilli glanced through a doorway to the right and saw a bedroom, decorated in white and black with touches of rose and gray. Behind her, reflected in the mirror, a well-equipped black and white kitchen with low granite counters glistened.

"Kate could've had a great career as a decorator," Lilli said.

"I'll pass along your compliment," Zack said. "Kate will be pleased." He shifted the weight of the suitcases. "Our rooms are upstairs. Come on, I'll show you around."

Lilli followed Zack up the winding staircase to the loft where a sitting area, furnished with a chintz-covered couch and chairs, overlooked the foyer. Lilli looked over the railing to the lower level. Sunlight shone through the wall of glass blocks framing the front door and splashed across the foyer floor, dominated by a bird in flight, formed from black and gray mosaic chips. Lilli thought about Kate in her wheelchair, choosing a pattern that symbolized the freedom to soar, to escape all limitations. Kate didn't wallow in self-pity. Kate was a fighter, not a victim.

"Wow!" Zack exclaimed. "Kate's new computer setup is really impressive." He set down the suitcases and strode to the alcove at the far end of the sitting area.

White painted bookcases, each about three feet wide and five feet high, flanked a computer station, complete with a rolling chair and pull-out desktop.

Zack checked out the computer, keyboard, scanner and printer. "Kate still has the same equipment, but now she has room to spread out," he said. "This part of the loft was a storage closet until Kate hired a carpenter to knock down the wall and install all this. She's talked about nothing else for weeks." He ran his hands along several shelves and peered behind the printer.

"What are you looking for?" Lilli asked.

"A lever. Apparently, a *hidden* lever. Building codes forced the carpenter to leave a crawl space between the studs for access to the air-conditioning ducts. Kate didn't want to look at a gaping hole on either side of her computer, so he built the two bookcases. Each is a unit that slides out on a track at the flick of a lever. The carpenter's the same guy who installed an elevator in the closet off the foyer." He pointed to the double doors at the top of the stairs. "The elevator delivers Kate right here to her computer." He gave the bookcase another quick swipe and shrugged. "Kate will have to show us the lever. Come on, let's get you settled."

"I wonder what that pile of fishnets and sponges is doing in the corner," Lilli said. "They look so out of place."

"One of Kate's projects. I'm sure we'll hear all about it." He pretended to complain, but again Lilli sensed that he was proud of every activity Kate tackled.

Lilli looked admiringly at the computer alcove and living area. "Kate has certainly created a lovely home and work space for herself. Maybe she can give me a few tips."

"I'm sure you two will hit it off," he said. "Opposites usually do."

Lilli was still contemplating that clashing thought as Zack set her suitcase in the first bedroom. "This one's yours," he said. "I always stay in the back bedroom. It's got a great view over the lanai roof of the backyard."

Lilli had hardly begun unpacking her T-shirts and shorts when Zack rapped lightly on her door. "Do you have a minute?"

"Sure."

"I'd like to tell you about the problem at work before Kate comes in." He leaned back against the doorframe. "Remember that case I was working on?"

Lilli nodded. "You said it got messy."

"My boss yanked me off because he thought I was taking it too personally. Before he transferred me to this case, he insisted I see the precinct's psychologist, Dr. Brecker. Dr. Barbara Brecker. I did. Mostly we talked about family stuff. Geez, I hate all that touchy-feely crap. It makes me squirm. Anyway, Dr. Brecker says I have unresolved issues with Kate related to her accident." He shrugged and raised his palms toward the ceiling, as if he doubted his own words. "She says the case made me finally react to Kate's disability. I thought I had put all that behind me and then, Bam! Things started to spin out of control."

"Come on, Zack." Lilli took his hand. "Let's sit down on the couch. Tell me what you mean, out of control."

"The robbery suspect we'd been doing surveillance on—" Zack swallowed hard "—slipped through our fingers, pulled off another string of robberies and…" He swallowed again. "The bastard put a bullet in a victim's spine. She was a young woman, a graduate student ready to leave for an archeological dig in Morocco, and now she'll be looking at a wheelchair for the rest of her life."

"I'm so sorry, Zack. That kind of brutality would be tough for any detective to deal with. But for you, it's got to be doubly painful. You've had to relive Kate's accident." She didn't know what else to say.

Zack rested his head in his hands and massaged his temples. "I said some things, made a few threats in a bar where my buddies and I unwind after work, threats about what I'd like to do to the suspect in the interrogation room. Word got back to my boss. He pulled me off the case. The last thing he said to me was, 'get down there to Tomoka Park, and don't screw up anything, or your days on the force are numbered.'"

"Zack—"

"I'm telling you all this for a reason. I want to warn you that things may get very tense between Kate and me. You saw how we snapped at each other. We weren't always like that."

"The accident changed your relationship," Lilli said.

Zack nodded. "Dr. Brecker claims there are some issues Kate and I never faced. She thinks confronting them could get my head on straight and allow me to do my police work in a more controlled manner. I told Kate on the telephone and—"

"What did she say?"

"Kate got real nervous. She acted like I'd opened a can of worms and a really rotten one had wriggled out."

"Zack—"

The front door banged open.

"We'll finish this later," Lilli said. She realized that her trip to Florida involved much more than poking around Tomoka Park. Zack and Kate's tangled relationship was at stake. Lilli wasn't sure exactly how she figured into any of this, but she admired Kate and was head over heels in love with Zack. If given the opportunity, she would willingly help them confront the issue that haunted Zack, and possibly Kate, too. It couldn't be so terrible that it could ruin their relationship. Lilli knew how strong the bond could be between a sister and brother. Her brother Pete was her best friend and, since childhood, her best ally in standing up to their strong-willed parents.

Lilli and Zack were descending the staircase as Kate rolled her chair into the foyer. "Dinner will be ready in an hour," she said. "Zack, don't worry. I haven't forgotten that drink I promised. And Lilli, I'll make you one, too."

"Can't wait," Zack said. He muttered to Lilli, "Misery loves company."

"Lilli, would you mind coming with me?" Kate asked. "There's something important we need to discuss."

"Sure," Lilli said. Kate's expression was serious and her tone forceful. Lilli had an uneasy feeling that Kate resented her and intended to speak her mind once Zack was out of earshot.

"The lanai, actually it's my studio, is a good place to talk," Kate said. She wheeled herself toward the fireplace.

Lilli followed. "Your condo is spectacular," she said.

"The floor plan is perfect for me." Kate turned right at the sliding glass doors. "While my guests sleep upstairs, I can come to my studio and paint. Inspiration has a habit of striking at sunrise."

Lilli couldn't believe her eyes as she stepped into Kate's studio. Stacks of canvases lined the walls between the glass doors that overlooked the lawn and wall of trees. Easels holding portraits, still lifes, garden scenes and children at play, all in various stages of progress, sat in the middle of the floor.

Kate flipped a switch and the entire room glowed with soft light. "I had the luma-light ceiling installed when I had the lanai added on," Kate said. Lighted panels arched up to the center of the ceiling where a fan whirred softly.

"Your work is beautiful," Lilli said. She leaned close and peered at a group of framed works. "You're Katherine Lee?" she asked, awed by the well-known artist's name written in the right-hand corner of the canvases. "I own one of your paintings!"

"You're kidding!" Kate's face lit up.

"It's true," Lilli said.

"Sit down and tell me about it."

Lilli dropped into the white leather chair, the only piece of furniture in the room. "Several years ago, when I sold my first freelance article, I decided to treat myself to something special. A few days later, I was at an art show in Greenwich Village—that's in New York City."

"Yes, I know where it is." Kate grinned. "I was there for the show's opening."

"Of course. Sorry. Anyway, I saw your painting and I had to have it."

"Which one, may I ask."

"The Cornfield," Kate said. "That little girl in an apron dress and sunbonnet hat holding onto her doll— she stole my heart. She stood there at the end of the field, taking in the world around her. You captured the innocence of childhood. I've tried to do that with my camera, but I've never succeeded. I can only imagine how difficult it must be."

"Thank you," Kate said. She thought for a few moments as if choosing her words. "I know Zack told you about my accident, that I landed in a cornfield."

Lilli nodded. "Now I understand the significance of the black storm clouds gathering over the cornstalks."

"Don't read too much into that," Kate said. "Storm clouds bring rain. The corn needs rain. Black clouds don't necessarily portray gloom. Things aren't ever that simple."

As they talked, Lilli agreed with Zack's assessment. Kate was an intelligent, complex, sensitive woman. She was already fond of Kate and wanted to know her better.

Kate moved her chair closer. "Zack has brought several women here to meet me. You're different from all the others. I predict you'll be around for a while."

"I hope so," Lilli said. She peered at Kate's painting again. "I still can't believe it. You're Katherine Lee."

"Yes," Kate said modestly. "I lead a somewhat schizophrenic life, and I like it that way. Katherine Lee, the artist, works here. Kate Faraday, the regular person who plays tennis, socializes with her friends and enjoys her brother's visits, relaxes here." The worry lines between her eyes grew deeper and the intensity of her gaze reminded Lilli of Zack. "I brought you to my studio because I want to set things straight."

Here it comes, Lilli thought, older sister protective of baby brother, wants to know…what, my intentions?

Kate's fingers folded and unfolded the hem of her tennis skirt. "You didn't have that look of pity I usually see when I meet people for the first time. That's good. I once allowed a journalist to interview me. When she arrived and opened her notebook, I saw that she had already entitled the story, 'The Day That Changed My Life Forever.' No matter what I said, she believed that everything in my life before the accident was wonderful, and after…well, let's just say she didn't see anything positive. She couldn't grasp that before the accident, I was an artists' agent, living in New York City, stressed out from promoting other people's careers, too busy to notice that I was burying my own talent."

Kate gnawed at her bottom lip. "I don't need to be-labor this. I just want you to know that I'm glad you're here. You can relax around me and treat me like a real person, who has good days and bad, good moods and bad. I'm not a China doll. I won't break."

"Promise?" Lilli asked and they both laughed.

"I know why you and Zack are here. He told me about the possible connection between Tomoka Park and the body in his precinct." Kate took a deep breath and Lilli wondered if she intended to comment on the police psychologist or possibly "the can of worms," as Zack called their unresolved issues regarding the accident.

The doorbell rang and Zack called out, "I'll get it." Lilli heard Zack say, "Mrs. D'Amato, how nice to see you."

"Come on," Kate said, propelling her chair into the living room. "You've got to meet Mrs. D'Amato, the sexy babe who lives in the other half of this building. Sometimes I think Zack comes to see her, not me!"

Lilli rushed to the foyer and let out a sigh of relief

as she shook hands with Mrs. D'Amato, a diminutive woman in her late sixties. She wore a black slinky gown with rhinestone straps and a long black chiffon scarf looped around her neck. Bright red lipstick accentuated her pale creamy skin, and a sleek bun at the nape of her swan-like neck emphasized her aristocratic cheekbones.

"Let me hear that heartbreaker high C," Zack said.

Mrs. D'Amato folded her hands, took a deep breath, tilted her chin toward the ceiling and sang with gusto, "do, re, mi, fa, so, la, ti, do!" She held the last note as the seconds on the clock ticked loudly. Lilli thought the mirrors and crystal chandelier would shatter.

Zack slid his arm around Mrs. D'Amato's waist. "Lilli, Mrs. D'Amato used to sing in the opera house in Milan. Now she's a local celebrity."

"That's right," Mrs. D'Amato said, "I sing in my cousin's restaurant—Luigi's Cantina—in the strip mall. Now I'm having fun with my music." She slid her scarf off her shoulder. "Also, I entertain at Italian grocery stores. Don't laugh. I sing my heart out while people push carts up and down the aisles scooping up fresh bread, oregano and olive oil. I don't mind if they talk or sing along or sample some of the sauce. I encourage them to enjoy life and they come back every week. The Christmas bonuses from my regulars are great! But let me come to the reason for my visit."

"To give me a thrill," Zack replied. "To make my day. To light up—"

Mrs. D'Amato snapped the end of her scarf at Zack's chin. "I was waiting in my foyer for Luigi to pick me up in his delivery truck. A big shiny car, midnight blue with lots of chrome, drove slowly around the cul-de-sac as if looking for a house number. It stopped in my driveway. I thought it was Luigi, playing the big spender, sending a fancy chauffeured limo for me. He's been acting like a big shot lately because he's going to present his award-winning mussels marinara at the VOCRA convention this weekend. VOCRA, that's the Volusia County Restaurant Association. So, where was I? Oh yes, the fancy blue car Luigi sent. I decided to play along. Doing my drop-dead diva impression, I swirled my scarf and sauntered down the driveway. I gave it my all—swiveled my hips, puckered my lips and threw kisses."

She blew a few kisses for effect. "Then I yanked open the door on the passenger side and, Mama Mia! I sure surprised the driver. He looked like he had tasted my mother-in-law's clam sauce, God rest her soul and her garlic press. He dropped his notepad and pen, floored the gas pedal and sped away. He left me standing in the dust. Actually he got dust all over my velvet shoes. I had to go back inside and scrub the rhinestone bows. Such disrespect! And for a diva, no less!"

"This is important, Mrs. D'Amato," Zack said taking her hands in his. "Did you notice his license plate number?"

"No."

"What did he look like?" Zack asked.

"A dark-haired guy, a northerner. You know, lots of khaki and brown. He had black hair slicked back in a ponytail."

"Could you identify him from a stack of photos?"

"Maybe. He has a tattoo."

"Where?"

"On his upper right arm. Something like a dragon's tail slithered down beneath his shirtsleeve."

"What do you suppose he was doing with the pen and paper?"

"Writing something down in a small notepad."

"Copying down my license plate number, perhaps?"

Mrs. D'Amato nodded. "Kate's, too, I'd say."

A car horn blasted. "That's Luigi," Mrs. D'Amato said. "I'll see you tomorrow night. You'll come to Luigi's Cantina with Kate and your new friend. Luigi will make his famous Veal Milanese. I'll sing 'That's Amore' just for you. And my cousins, Alfredo and Fettucini, that's their new professional name, I wanted something more tasteful, but they said 'what tastes better than fettucini alfredo?' Anyway, they'll accompany me on the guitar and mandolin. See you there." She floated toward the door, her scarf trailing across the mosaic bird.

Before the door closed, Zack was punching in numbers on his cell phone. "Trouble, boss. Somebody knows I'm here. Touch base with the local powers and have them send two detectives over here. Right away." He narrowed his eyes. "Make sure one of them is Lobo Cruz. I know him. He's their best."

FOUR

Tomoka Park

A STREAM OF MOTORCYCLES wove through the cars as
Lilli and Zack headed into the glaring morning sunshine toward Ormond Beach. Ahead of their car, the
bikers' lacquered helmets formed an intricate pattern
of primary colors with flecks of gold and shiny black.
The pattern reminded Lilli of the Timucua legends she'd
seen woven into necklaces in the brochures Kate had
left on her night table.

Woven patterns. Hmmm. That old phrase, 'Oh what
a tangled web we weave when first we practice to de-
ceive,' came to mind. But what deceit was happening
here? Lilli wondered. She had agreed with Zack to
postpone any talk of his problems. They would focus
on the Tomoka Park investigation, but make time for
her photographs and interviews. There were no hints of
any unpleasant confrontation between Zack and Kate.
The blue sedan had not returned. Two detectives had
arrived, as Zack requested. And Zack had checked in
with the Ormond Beach Police Department. Although
they weren't thrilled to have a New Yorker invade their
territory, they had been civil.

"Detective Lobo Cruz is the perfect guy to watch over my sister," Zack said and relaxed his grip on the steering wheel. "I met Lobo and some of his buddies at the Ormond Beach Recreation Center. When I'm in town, I join in their Monday night basketball game. It's a good workout. I sized up Lobo last night as he checked out the security system and talked to Kate. He's thorough and he's taking things seriously."

Lilli pictured Lobo Cruz with his tanned complexion, cropped black hair and the faint dimples that flashed when he smiled. "Lobo, the wolf," Lilli mused. "His name suits him. Did you see the way he wolfed down Kate's chicken curry and Mrs. D'Amato's kiwi tarts?"

"Good thing there's no full moon this week. The residents might not appreciate his howling." Zack's handsome faced turned serious. "Lobo's credentials are impressive. A wrestling scholarship at the University of Central Florida, a black belt in karate and good communication skills in English and Spanish. And, as I've found out, one heck of a basketball player."

Zack sped up to lose a tailgating motorcyclist. "His partner, Jones, is no slouch either. Mrs. D'Amato finally agreed he could camp out at her place. She figures a plainclothed detective with a dull name like John Jones probably eats oatmeal for breakfast, lunch and dinner. She threatened to spice up his life, and I hesitate to think what she has in mind."

"Sounds like she has more than extra pepper flakes in his spaghetti sauce planned," Lilli joked. "But John

Jones may surprise her. Still waters run deep, they say, and I saw the way he looked at Kate and her paintings. He appreciates beauty. By the way, what did Mrs. D'Amato whisper to you when we left?"

"She complained that I gave the cute detective to Kate. She doesn't want to hear that Lobo is a family man with a wife and three kids."

Lilli laughed and sank back in her seat. "What a day Lobo and John are in for. Kate says Mrs. D'Amato spends all morning practicing her scales *espressivo* and pounding the piano *fortissimo*. And Kate plans to start a new painting which she figures Vivaldi's booming crescendos will inspire. Those men won't be able to hear themselves think, let alone concentrate on their paperwork."

Zack adjusted the rearview mirror. "Kate and Mrs. D'Amato will get their undivided attention. We can poke around Tomoka State Park and not worry about them."

Lilli heard the catch in Zack's voice and knew that he was trying to convince himself.

Zack honked his horn impatiently at a slow driver. "Once we get to the park, I can start asking questions, discreetly of course, about Benjamin Voda, while we pretend to be tourists. Someone will remember him, I'm sure of it. I'm hoping they can describe anyone he was with."

"Aren't you forgetting something?" Lilli asked.

"We're not just tourists. We're a happy couple intrigued by each other."

"Right," Zack said.

Slowing down, they passed several shops in the three-block downtown district. "Let's come back and explore this street. It's so quaint," Lilli said.

Zack chuckled. "Not as quaint as the shopkeepers."

"The Corner Book Store…Ormond Treasures… Thrifty Threads…Bud's Blooms." Lilli's head turned side to side like windshield wipers as she rattled off the names painted on the windows and awnings of the silver-gray buildings with pristine white trim.

"There's Betty's Pet Shop," Zack said. "You met Betty, Kate's tennis friend." Zack pointed toward the turnoff to the right. "Sad to say, the scene of Benjamin Voda's bloody shootout took place only minutes from here. The gas station where he holed up is at the first light."

Lilli glimpsed an empty road as far as she could see. "I guess no one likes to travel that road any more."

"Too many bad memories." He changed lanes. "We can't erase the past," he said. "But we can try to stop the same carnage from happening again with illegal guns Voda probably supplied to buyers." Zack gritted his teeth. "I'd give anything to pick up his trail in Tomoka Park and follow it to his customers. This town deserves some peace and quiet."

Several motorcycles roared past and Zack laughed

at the irony of his words. "Okay, maybe not peace and quiet. Let's just say there should be better days ahead."

Lilli admired Zack's professional dedication, his resolve to eliminate trouble before it started. She thought the New York City Police Department was lucky to have him. But it was his basic goodness that was most appealing. Zack simply wanted to shape a better life for Kate and the people of Ormond Beach. She felt extremely fortunate that he had come into her life.

Zack turned north at the bridge that crossed the Halifax River and brought visitors to motels and high-rise condos on the beach. "There will be less traffic here on North Beach Street," Zack said, following a straggling line of dusty bikers. "We'll be at Tomoka State Park in ten minutes."

Lilli glanced over her shoulder at the downtown district. "This is great," she said, noticing that most of the bikers had circled around and were now following close behind. She grabbed her camera. Planting her hiking boots in the middle of her seat, she poked her head and shoulders through the sunroof and snapped away. "Do you suppose all these bikers are going to Tomoka Park, too?" she shouted to Zack.

"You bet. They all want to meet one gorgeous photographer," he said, careful to maintain a steady speed and not spoil her photos.

Lilli smiled and enjoyed Zack's compliment. Back in her seat, Lilli commented, "Kate is very thoughtful.

She left a packet of information about Tomoka Park on my night table."

Zack followed the narrow road, which meandered along the river. "Good. I've never been to the park. I did some research when the Tomoka connection was first made, but I looked for evidence of crime, like industrial cover-up of the dumping of toxic waste, or…well, you get my point."

Lilli nodded. "Kate's information is more historical and cultural. She underlined the paragraph about the French artist, Jacques le Moyne, who created a series of engravings and commentaries about the Timucua Indians and their way of life in the mid-fifteen-hundreds. She wrote in the margin that copies of the engravings and commentaries are available at the local library. She thought that as a photojournalist, I would enjoy them. Sounds good, don't you think?"

"Yes, but be prepared for a sad story. There were forty thousand Timucua spread across northern Florida before the European explorers arrived. Fighting, disease and the evils of colonialism claimed every last one of them."

"Teh-mook-kwa," Lilli said, allowing the syllables to linger on her lips. "Teh-mook-kwa. According to the brochures their beautiful and mysterious-sounding name means 'lord and chief' or 'my enemy.' What happened to them is a shame." Lilli was still thinking about the fate of the Timucua when she noticed the string of road signs advertising Indigo Condominiums, Indigo Apartments and the new Indigo Mall. "Indigo sure is a big name around here," she remarked.

"Do you remember my mentioning that the body in New York had traces of indigo on the skin? Before leaving New York, I researched indigo on the internet. There's a notebook in my gym bag, if you'd like to check out the information."

Lilli reached into the back seat, rummaged around in Zack's bag and pulled out the notebook. Flipping past pages labeled 'local industries,' 'police officers in Ormond Beach and Daytona,' 'Tomoka State Park' and 'Benjamin Voda's rampage,' she found Zack's entry for indigo, a computer printout stapled to the page.

Lilli read out loud, "In 1764, Richard Oswald, a Scottish merchant, West Indies planter, slave trader and friend of the British court, received twenty thousand acres from the English Privy Council. Governor Grant, British Governor of East Florida, chose the land for Oswald in what is today's Tomoka State Park area because it was well situated on a river, one of Oswald's requirements. Oswald purchased about fifty slaves from South Carolina, most of them experienced in making indigo dye. He turned indigo plants into a lucrative cash crop at his plantation, Mount Oswald. Indigo was in demand for body paint, tinting clay for ceramics and dyeing fabrics, including the uniforms for General Washington's soldiers and later, the trousers for the Confederate soldiers. After the big land rush that followed the Civil War, everyone out west ordered indigo from the east, and the indigo industry thrived. Once Levi Strauss created his famous blue work pants, the industry really boomed."

Lilli smoothed her cut-off jeans and noticed that Zack wore a denim shirt. Some styles never die, she thought and studied the information. "Zack, could there be a connection between the present-day indigo industry and the dead man, like industrial dumping or river pollution?"

"I doubt it. Keep reading and you'll see what happened."

Lilli turned the page. "Eventually a synthetic substitute for indigo was discovered and the discoverer, Adolph Von Baeyer, won the Nobel Prize in 1905."

Lilli closed the notebook. "Darn! I thought indigo was going to crack your case wide open. Then we could spend our time swimming and relaxing."

"I like your concept of police work," Zack quipped.

They continued along North Beach Street, slowing down as the road narrowed and passing beneath a canopy of oak trees. Lilli felt as if she were leaving civilization and entering the forest primeval. Tall trees blocked out the sun. The vegetation grew thick and wild and the faint odor of decaying mulch diminished the fragrance of pine needles. They stopped at the ticket booth. A large bulletin board with the words 'Tomoka Remembers' arched across the top featured snapshots of weaving, dyeing, basket making and historical reenactments.

"Welcome," the pudgy-faced ticket taker said, batting

her eyelids aglow with green eyeshadow. "You're in luck," she said, accepting Zack's ticket money. "Today's the second Saturday of the month, so we're staging another Tomoka Remembers." Handing over change along with several brochures, she lowered her face into the car window. "Take my advice, Tootsie," she said to Lilli. "Don't let the Timucua maiden in the teeny-weeny bikini steal your man."

"Where exactly is this maiden?" Zack asked and Lilli shot him a frosty glance.

Zack paced himself behind the bikers who surprisingly obeyed the five-mile-an-hour speed limit. "We'll have to move faster than this to talk to the park ranger, grounds people, maintenance people and anyone else who's been here on a regular basis."

"Especially if you want time with the Timucua maiden," Lilli said.

Zack chuckled and proceeded through groves of stiff-leafed palmettos and dagger-tipped yucca that rattled in the breeze. Here and there red, pink, yellow and white blossoms poked through the greenery. Lilli thought she spotted several orchids among the more common flowers. She reached up through the sunroof and caught one of the strands of silvery green Spanish moss that dangled from the pine branches. "According to the brochures, the Timucua women draped the Spanish moss across their bodies, sort of like a skirt."

"I wonder if that's what the Timucua maiden's bikini is made from," Zack said.

"Men," Lilli muttered.

"The boat launch area is over there," Zack said, veering to the left. He pulled into the clearing and circled past the picnic tables nestled beneath a rustic shelter roof. Couples carrying lightweight aluminum canoes walked past a line of rental airboats and kayaks and strode to the water's edge. Several boaters were already paddling down the river toward the far end of the park. "Anyone could come in here by boat after the park closes," Zack said.

"On foot, too," Lilli said. "The park isn't fenced, and I didn't see any signs that it's patrolled."

Zack cupped his hands. "How's the fishing?" he called out.

A guy wearing an 'I love Florida' T-shirt waved. "The trout are running good."

Lilli gazed at the wide river and the distant riverbank. "How about a canoe trip this afternoon, Zack? We should explore the area from the water. A change of perspective works wonders for photographers."

"For detectives, too," Zack said, gazing into her eyes.

They had been back in the car only a few minutes when Lilli saw a sign: Registered Campers Only. Next to it, someone had hammered a stake into the ground, nailed a cardboard sign to the stake and printed in large black letters: Biker Camp.

"So that explains why the bikers are here in droves," Lilli said, checking her film. "They sleep in the park during Bike Week. This will be out first stop. I just know there's a story here. A story that *Viewpoint* readers will never forget."

"That's what scares me," Zack said and shot Lilli a look that sent a chill up her spine.

FIVE

Heaven

LILLI AND ZACK HOPPED out of the car and headed down the path through the pine trees toward biker camp. Lilli expected to find a scene from her childhood summers, basic khaki-brown camping tents, pit fires, rusty bicycles and ropes lined with dripping clothes strung between trees.

"Wow!" she exclaimed, gazing at the huge motor homes complete with satellite dishes, enormous barbecue grills with monogrammed covers and fancy umbrellas shading picnic tables. "Those homes must cost at least a hundred thousand dollars each, and their tents are amazing. Look at those white dome-shaped ones perched on wooden platforms. They look like igloos that took flight, migrated from the North Pole and landed in Florida."

Zack whistled through his teeth as he peered at dozens of Harleys. Black predominated, but here and there an aqua, yellow or red one glistened in the filtering light. "Their bikes must go for forty thousand dollars and more. What the heck do these guys do for a living?"

"From what I've read, many are accountants, doctors and lawyers," Lilli said. "But they come from all walks of life. I guess the camaraderie develops from their mutual love of the open highway."

"And the crowded park," Zack quipped.

When Lilli and Zack walked by, several bikers looked up from shaking frying pans on their grills or sipping coffee and waved. "Hi," and "hey," they said. "Howdy," and "how y'all doin'?" they called out.

"Hello," Lilli said to a burly full-bearded biker who lumbered out of his motor home. He pointed one thumb at his massive chest and lifted the other thumb in a victory salute. Lilli could tell from the other bikers' nods and thumbs-up that they knew he had everything under control. Besides the typical jeans and leather, he wore a cowboy hat adorned with brown and black speckled feathers that arched toward his back.

"I hope we're not imposing or trespassing," Lilli said, "but I'd like to photograph the camp and interview some of the bikers for *Viewpoint* magazine. I'm Lilli and this is Zack."

"Well, little lady, you and your old man have picked the best spot in biker camp." He shook their hands and his feathers danced. "My name's Billy Bob and this here section where you're standing is Harley Heaven. Take all the photos you want, on one condition."

"I'm listening," Lilli said.

"Promise you'll mention our Parade of Toys and other

charitable causes. Give us a fair shake, that's all me and my friends ask."

"You got yourself a deal," Lilli exclaimed and began snapping photos of the motor homes and tents.

Billy Bob ran his hands back and forth along the handlebars of the bike by his side. "You'll want to know about our bikes. We've got Harley Superglides and Low-Riders, Harley Heritages and Sportsters."

Snap! Snap! Lilli snapped photos as fast as Billy Bob pointed out the bikes. Zack jotted down the names in Lilli's notebook.

"Harley Wideglides. Custom colors and designs."

Snap! Snap!

"And, right here, my Harley Davidson Road King with thunder cones and the original mufflers."

Snap! Snap! Lilli had never seen so much chrome.

"Beyond Harley Heaven—" Billy Bob's arms swept to the right "—there's purgatory. Don't get me wrong, there are some mighty fine bikes over there, but them boys is just passing time until they can own the real thing."

"A Harley," Lilli said to let him know she was following.

"Then, of course, there's hell." Billy Bob's arms swept to the right, beyond where he said purgatory was located. He shook his head. "The bikes and bikers from hell give us a bad name. No polish, no pride. No shine, no shame. Now, little lady, how can I help you without irritating your old man who's fidgeting to move on?"

"Give me a minute, Billy Bob," Lilli said and pulled Zack aside. "Go ahead and find out what you can and give me some time with Billy Bob. I can get an article on bikers. And since Billy Bob's the leader of the pack and willing to talk, something might turn up that could help your investigation."

"I don't think your being here alone is a good idea," Zack protested.

"I'll be fine," she insisted.

Billy Bob leaned forward. "You can trust me, ole buddy. Harley people are honorable. Harley Heaven is just like it says, heaven on earth, and we won't do nothing to tarnish our reputation."

Zack poked the leaves with the toe of his running shoe and looked at Lilli's pleading eyes. "Take good care of my little woman," Zack said shaking Billy Bob's hand. "I'll be back in an hour."

"Thanks," Lilli said and pecked Zack on the cheek.

"Hold on, Zack, ole buddy." Billy Bob fished a business card from his pocket and handed it to Zack. "Come see me some time. Billy Bob's Boots in Ocala. I'll fix you up with a pair of eelskins, top of the line, just like mine." He stuck out his left boot, lifted the pointed toe knee-high, and hopped forward on his right foot, like he was doing some weird dance. "Them running shoes of yours have seen their best days. Let me boot you up. And then you can pay a visit to my little woman. She's in the hat business." He ran his fingertips up his hat feathers. "One of her hats has your name on it."

Zack waved the business card. "Thanks, Billy Bob. I look forward to a new image." As Zack walked away, Billy Bob tipped his hat and said, "Now, little lady, let's get to your story."

"I always work with a theme," Lilli began. "That's how I tie everything together."

"My little woman's the same way," Billy Bob said. "Peacock feathers got to have a blue or green hat band. Speckled feathers like mine, brown or black band. Stubbornest woman I ever met. Well, your time's frittering away. What kind of theme you got in mind?"

"Night and Day," Lilli said. "Bikers enjoying barreling down the highway during the day, relaxing in biker camp at night. What do you think?"

"Just like my boots, it's got class. You're welcome here any time, even after dark, so you can get the full picture. We'd be pleased to have you and your old man join us for a late supper. Let's say eight o'clock? We've got some gourmet cooks in the crowd."

"Thanks. We'll be there," Lilli said, "but there's something else I need."

"Name it. I'll do anything to get some good publicity for me and my buddies."

"Every story needs a dash of drama. Has there ever been any trouble in the park? You know, something mysterious that would spice up this setting."

"The legend of the Tomoka Lights is just what you're looking for."

Lilli moved the microphone closer to Billy Bob. "Go on."

"It's a ghosty-ghouly fog that slithers like an alligator across the marsh after dark. It leaves people all shook up."

Lilli shuddered. "Please tell me there's a logical explanation."

"Some folks say it's swamp gas, released as car headlights hit it. Old timers around here tell that it rushes toward you and...*ssssshwoooom!*...you're out the other side, scared and shaking."

"Where does all this happen?"

"Yonder—" Billy Bob pointed in the direction Zack had gone "—at the old wooden bridge, Lovers' Bridge, locals call it. It was replaced years ago."

"I hope Zack and I can see the lights when we come back tonight."

"You're out of luck, little lady. The story goes there was a couple making out in a parked car. Another car trying to avoid the lights crashed into the lovers' car and those darned lights ain't been seen since."

"That's a good legend, but I could use something spicier."

"I'd think us bikers would be spicy enough, but how about a dead body or two?"

"Now you're talking." Lilli couldn't believe her good fortune.

Billy Bob's eyes glistened. "The park ranger found

a two-hundred-year-old skull buried in a shallow at the north point of the park."

"Anything else?" Lilli said encouragingly.

"During prohibition a body was found buried head first with his shoes sticking out of the mud. Some rum-runners from the sugar cane industry at the Bulow Plantation Ruins, down the road apiece, shipped their moonshine to the Caribbean islands. Some bodied turned up back then. Yeah, this area has seen its share of bodies."

"Bulow Plantation Ruins?" Lilli asked.

"It's real popular with tourists. A visit to Tomoka Park and Bulow Plantation makes for a nice weekend."

Lilli wondered if the dead man in New York City had visited Bulow Plantation. She would mention the possibility to Zack. "Do you remember anything more recent here in this park?"

Billy Bob nodded. "Some drug deals went bad a few years ago just after Bike Week. A young woman hanging out with a rough crowd turned up dead, buried in leaves and mulch."

Lilli heard men's voice. Someone shouted, "Hey, Billy Bob! Guys! Give us a hand! This guy's been attacked."

Lilli looked up and saw Zack, his arms draped across the shoulders of two bikers who were helping him toward a lounge chair.

"Zack! What happened?" Lilli cried, rushing to his side.

"I'm fine," Zack said collapsing into the chair. "Just give me a few minutes to clear my head." Lilli held his hand and knelt by his side. The dozen bikers who gathered around offered him water, eggs and bacon, a pillow for his head.

"I'll be on my feet in a minute," Zack insisted. He whispered to Lilli, "Someone broke the car window, dumped my gym bag and stole my notebook. We need to get away from here so I can call Lobo in private."

"Make way for the medics!" Billy Bob exclaimed, clearing a path for three bikers who rushed forward carrying little black leather bags. "Fear not, little lady, we know the drill," Billy Bob said reassuringly to Lilli. "Zack, ole buddy, this is Dr. Crespi, a neurosurgeon, and this here's Dr. Preston, a cardiologist. Enthusiastic fellows, eager to evaluate, prescribe,and operate, but given the present circumstances, they're not for you." He elbowed them out of the way. "Allow me to introduce Mr. Alan White." He ushered the short, rotund man with a three-day stubble toward Zack. "Dr. White operates a walk-in clinic in St. Petersburg."

Dr. White looked down his nose at the other doctors, mumbled something about specialization, and then turned his attention to Zack. "What hurts?" he asked, checking Zack's eyes, ears, nose and mouth.

"My head and shoulder," Zack said. Lilli helped the doctor remove Zack's shirt. He winced when the doctor touched his left shoulder and Lilli saw a large red welt forming.

"Who did this to you?" Lilli asked.

"I don't know. When I got to our car I saw right away that the tire was flat. I was getting the jack and spare out of the trunk when I heard a branch snap behind me. I turned. The guy, whoever he was, lunged. I ducked, tripped and slammed into the bumper. Next thing I know, these two guys came along." He pointed to the bikers.

"You're a lucky man, Zack," Dr. White said and snapped his bag shut.

"To be alive?"

"No, to have the prettiest woman for miles around." Everyone laughed and Lilli blushed. "Just checking your reactions," Dr. White admitted. "I'm sure you'll be fine." He said to Lilli, "When you leave here, make sure he sees a doctor for tests and X-rays."

"Thank you, doctor," Lilli said.

"Don't worry, Zack," the tallest biker said. "Harry stayed behind to change your tire and he's keeping an eye on your car. What was the guy's beef with you?"

"I don't have a clue," Zack said and squeezed Lilli's hand.

Lilli tapped Zack playfully with her fist. "Are you sure it wasn't the Timucua maiden? I hear she always gets her man."

"Yeah," said Billy Bob. "Just like Cupid, with an arrow straight to the heart. Or in this case, a bumper straight to the shoulder."

SIX

Tomoka Remembers

ZACK FUMED. "The guy who stole my notebook will see the stuff about Voda. That hinders my being here for vacation reasons. We'll have to move faster than I'd thought." He eased the car onto the road toward the park's visitor center. "I'm convinced the guy who stole my notebook is the same guy Mrs. D'Amato saw in front of Kate's condo."

"What makes you say that?" Lilli asked.

"I caught a glimpse of a tall guy who fits her description—dark clothes, ponytail and a tattoo on his right arm—but I didn't see his face. My guess? He probably knows *who* we are. He could have checked that out through the airline or car rental, but he figured the notebook would reveal *why* we're here. Are we vacationing? Am I tagging along on your photo shoot? Or do we have other more compelling reasons?"

Zack pulled up to the visitor center and parked beneath a pine tree. "I'd like to think that there's such a mixture of local and historical information in the notebook besides a general run-down on Voda, that our plans aren't completely transparent."

"It's possible," Lilli said. "Any vacationing cop would be interested in Voda."

"And any photojournalist would delve into local history."

"But why the flat tire?" Lilli asked.

"Probably to slow us down."

"I'll buy that," Lilli said. "But attacking you seems unnecessary, unless he's just plain vicious."

"My hunch is he saw me coming back before he had a chance to break into the car, and he hid in the bushes. After I crashed into the bumper and lay there in a daze, I remember hearing the sound of shattering glass. That must be when he broke the window, dumped my gym bag and stole the notebook. I don't think his original plan was to hurt me. That would call too much attention, something I'm sure he'd rather have avoided. I think you'd better go back to Kate's and stay there with Lobo. If my hunch about this guy is wrong and he does intend to harm us, your life could be in danger."

"Danger is part of my work as a photojournalist," Lilli said.

"I can't put you in harm's way. That was never part of our deal."

"I'm staying with you," Lilli protested. "I have no intention of giving up this photo shoot."

"But—"

"This is a once-in-a-lifetime chance. We'll be okay."

"But—"

"You were alone. If we stay where there are lots of visitors, he won't dare try again."

"But—"

"I'm sure the bikers would help us. Please?"

"Okay, but promise you'll be careful." Zack exhaled as if he'd just finished a marathon. "Geez! We sound like an old married couple deciding who's the boss."

"Zack, that's so cute. And what conclusion did you draw?"

"Hmmmmmmm." Zack pulled out his cell phone and punched in numbers. "Kate, it's Zack. I need to speak to Lobo. Busy, doing what?" He listened for a few seconds and then burst out laughing. He winked at Lilli. "Lobo's entertaining Kate with a Spanish version of Abbott and Costello's routine, 'who's on first, what's on second.' According to Lobo, it's 'Julio's on first, Juan's on second.'"

Zack turned back to the phone. "Hey, Lobo, our suspect followed us here. He stole my notebook and it probably gave him some clues about why I'm here. He might try and break into Kate's condo and snoop around. Have your people come up with any matches on the tattoo based on Mrs. D'Amato's description?… Well, let me know and stay sharp. Right, right. Thanks. Talk to you later." He turned to Lilli. "Lobo's got everything under control. Let's see if there's anyone in charge of the visitor center. They might remember seeing Voda here at sometime."

Lilli looked over her shoulder as she stepped away

from the car. She had a jittery feeling that she and Zack were being followed. She didn't say anything to Zack because he would insist that she leave.

Entering the sprawling rustic building, Lilli called out, "Hello!" Her voice echoed around the cinderblock walls and wood ceiling. "There's a museum here, too," she said. "Let's see if someone's on duty."

"Good idea," Zack said. "They might know something that could connect Voda to this park."

Lilli led the way past the dioramas of saltwater lagoons, cypress ponds, beaches and barrier islands into the next room where display cases exhibited stone, shell and bone weapons. "Strange that no one's here," she said, peering into the cases at the Timucua clay pots from the Orange Period, St. Johns Period I and II and St. Augustine Period. She turned the corner and gasped. A black bear standing on its hind legs stared her down.

"He sure looks real," Zack marveled.

"Yes, and so do some of the other animals. Check out the bobcat and deer. Their glassy eyes give me the willies."

They walked down a long corridor lined with huge plaques of Timucua warriors, whose long hair tied up in a topknot made an ideal quiver for arrows. Aided by the artist's fantasy, brave warriors confronted a group of landroving crocodiles, jammed sticks down their throats, flipped them onto their backs, shot arrows into their soft bellies and clubbed them to death. A hunting party, lurking beneath deer hides and heads, stalked white-tail deer. A war party slaughtered a rival tribe and set fire to their village. Several braves raised a ceremonial deer's head decorated with wildflowers, offering it to the sun.

The sound of metal scraping metal stopped Lilli in her tracks.

"Hello! Anyone there?" Zack called out.

Silence.

"This could be our man and I aim to catch him," Zack whispered. He took the lead and motioned Lilli forward.

There was that scraping noise again! And it was louder than before.

Zack touched Lilli's arm, signaling her to stay back. He peered around the long, low case where a dugout canoe rested on a pebble-lined shore. "Just the breeze," Zack said and Lilli added, "The breeze and our active imaginations." She saw the back door swing back and forth on its hinges.

"All the tourists and park people must be at the craft demonstrations," Zack said. "That's where we should go."

"Do you mind waiting a few minutes? I'd like some photos of the miniature Timucua village in the case along the back wall. What a great contrast that will make with my biker camp photos. I won't be long." She reached into her tote bag for her camera with the best flash capability. "Oh darn! I left the extra film for this camera in the car. I only have a dozen shots left on the roll."

"I'll get it," Zack said. "Be back in a flash!"

"That's a real old photographers' joke," Lilli teased and quickly set to work. Standing on tiptoes, she shot down through the top of the case at the stockade surrounding the crop fields, mounds and temple. Then she zoomed in for the circular thatched huts, village kitchen, granaries, elevated on stakes and racks where deer, fish, snakes and lizards smoked over a fire pit.

Lilli stepped back to check on the glare from the glass before photographing the chief's elaborate home. She froze. A reflection in the glass! A man stood right behind her! He had a ponytail and wore a black muscle shirt. Tattoos adorned both of his arms. She spun toward him, the light from her flash repeating as she clicked furiously. "Help! Zack! Help me!" she shouted and kicked the man in the shin as hard as she could.

"Gawl dang it!" the man hollered, hopping on one foot and rubbing his eyes. "You trying to break my leg and blind me, all at the same time?"

Lilli blinked and rubbed her eyes. "Oh, I'm so sorry!" She recognized him as one of the bikers who had helped Zack. "You startled me."

"That's what *I* was about to say. Anyway, my name's Russell. I saw you come in here and just wanted to say, if Billy Bob don't feed you good vittles, come to my campsite, just three spots from his. Sorry if I scared you."

"Lilli! Lilli!" Zack dashed past the dugout canoe and charged into the room. He stopped short, gasping for breath, when he saw Lilli smiling and talking to Russell.

"Sorry," Lilli said sheepishly. "My nerves are jangled. Too much caffeine this morning, I guess." She didn't want to say too much in front of Russell. Zack didn't want anyone to know they were in the park on a police matter.

"See you tonight," Russell said. He passed Zack and mumbled, "A real spitfire of a woman you got yourself, ole buddy. I'd take her in a heartbeat."

"OUR FIRST STOP, THE INDIGO dye maker," Zack said as he studied the visitors' map. He and Lilli ducked beneath the pine branches and joined the crowd listening to a petite blonde in a ruffled cap and ankle-length calico dress. As she talked, she stirred the dye bath bubbling in a cauldron and scooped up the yarn with a stick. Zack confided to Lilli, "I think she taught Kate how to make her herbal brews."

Lilli took a photograph of the woman as she draped the vivid blue yarn over a clothesline strung between two oak trees. Then Lilli zoomed in on a group of children who shifted from foot to foot and listened half-heartedly as the dye maker explained, "The Timucua Indians soaked indigo plants releasing indoxyl, the dye-making ingredient. The clever Timucua discovered that they could speed up the process by adding urine to the water."

A freckle-faced boy tugged at his cowlick. "You mean the Indians peed in this pot?"

"Why yes, I suppose so. I mean no, not this very pot. They peed in their own pots." She looked flustered and waved forward six Timucua braves. Lilli glanced at the program and saw that they were members of the Ormond Beach High School wrestling team. Composing herself, the dyemaker continued, "The elite, such as Chief Outina and Chief Potano—" she pointed to the first two braves, who preened like peacocks "—used indigo and other natural dyes to decorate their bodies."

The chiefs, in full body paint, flexed their biceps and strutted for the cheering crowd. With fierce eyes and firm jaws, they posed with bows and arrows. Slinging their weapons aside, Chief Outina wrestled Chief Potano long and hard before finally pinning him to the ground. The four braves lifted the victorious Chief Outina onto a platform and marched back and forth. When several teenage girls elbowed their way forward for a better view, Lilli caught their awed expressions on film. She smiled at the girls' frisky antics, similar to behavior she'd seen at concerts, and remembered with a hint of nostalgia her own raging teenage hormones. Come to think of it, since meeting Zack Faraday, her hormones were once again deliriously out of control.

Lilli began to relax and enjoy herself. She realized she might have overreacted in the museum. This was

Florida, land of fun and sunshine. Make the most of it, she told herself. If trouble came, she'd know it. So would Zack. And a cry for help would certainly draw the crowd's attention. The bikers had helped before. They could be counted on again.

A thunderous round of drumming startled Lilli and the crowd began to disperse. "What's going on?" she asked a stoop-shouldered man who brushed past her.

"The Tomokie Legend reenactment is starting in fifteen minutes," he said. "Today's maiden is a regular and verrrrrry popular."

"Give me a few minutes, Lilli. I want to ask the dye maker and braves some questions. Maybe they'll remember that Voda had visited the park." Zack strode away toward the dye maker.

Lilli knelt down and began packing her cameras into her tote bag. She was suddenly aware of someone standing over her. "Need some assistance, madam?"

Looking up, Lilli cupped her hand over her eyes to block the sun's rays. "No thanks," she said, squinting up at the man's impeccably tailored slacks and shirt and handsome face.

"You appear to be a professional photographer," he said, his voice hinting at a foreign accent that Lilli couldn't place. "Working on a special assignment?" he asked, helping her to her feet.

Lilli's breath caught in her throat. A tattoo snaked down his right arm! An embossed silver band clasped his ponytail. This has to be the man following us, Lilli thought. She would buy some time, engage him in conversation, keep him by her side until Zack returned. "No, the assignment isn't very special," she said surprised at the calmness of her voice. "Just your typical tourist stuff."

"Looks like a big job to me," he said, patting her bulging tote bag.

"Not really." The guy was fishing for information, just like Zack figured. Well, she'd throw him off the track. When Zack returned, she'd get his attention and signal him to play along. "Actually I'm bored with this shoot," Lilli said. "I'll probably leave today and drive to Orlando's theme parks."

The man nodded toward Zack who was laughing and talking with the braves. "Your assistant seems to be enjoying an amusing story from the actors."

"Oh he's not my assistant. He's my uh, significant other, and lucky him, he has excess vacation time to squander. So, you know, use it or lose it. While I work, he plays. What a deal!" Lilli chuckled, trying to buy time, and heard her chuckle become a high-pitched twitter. "He's talking to the warriors because he's thinking about getting a tattoo, something exotic…" she brazenly pushed up his sleeve "…like yours."

Whoa! The tattoo was entwined stems and a single blossom. Flowers, for gosh sakes, not a dragon's tail like she'd expected. "Definitely a tattoo like yours," Lilli said and forced a smile, which she sensed was turning into a frozen ear-to-ear grin.

From the corner of her eye, Lilli saw Zack striding toward her. "Come meet my new friend," she called out, pulling off her glasses, blinking her eyes like crazy, hoping to catch Zack's attention and alert him that something important to the investigation was going down. "He has a tattoo you should see."

"Sorry," the man said brusquely. "I'm late for an appointment." He turned, ducked beneath the pine branches and was gone.

Lilli grabbed Zack's hand, turned him around, and marched him toward the dye maker and braves. "Just keep walking. Don't ask any questions. And, whatever you do, don't look back at the pine trees."

Zack shook his head. "What's with the shrewish wife and hen-pecked husband routine? I thought our plan was to behave like two people in love."

"Knock off the wisecracks," Lilli said and snapped a few photos. "Okay, we can go now." She steered him toward the pine trees and their car.

"Good," he said checking his watch, "because the braves said if I want to see what's really happening in this park, I should go to the Tomokie Legend reenactment. Come on. We don't want to be late."

Once inside their car, Lilli said, "Start the engine and drive."

"Yes, dear!" Zack said, pretending meekness, and turned the key in the ignition. He drove a few yards and jammed down the brake pedal. "Do you mind telling me what the heck's going on?"

Lilli took a deep breath. "I spoke with the guy who attacked you."

"You what? Where is he?" Zack grabbed the door handle.

"Sit back and listen. If you go after him, he'll know you're here on police business. He's watching us, I'm sure of it. I'll bet he was lurking around the museum, but that big biker, Russell, came along and scared him off."

Zack slammed his fists on the steering wheel. "Are you completely out of your mind?"

"I think I convinced the creep that I'm working on an assignment and you're on vacation. Oh, by the way, the tattoo isn't a snake or dragon's tail. It's an orchid with fancy curlicue stems."

"Don't ever play detective again. Do you hear me?" Zack leaned toward her, eyes blazing. "He could be dangerous. He could have hurt you."

"Only if he thinks we're here on police business."

"Listen, Lilli. Stick to photography. Leave the police work to me."

"Think about this. Why is he so intent on finding out what we're doing here at the park? Because this is where the action is. Something bad is going to happen here soon. All we have to do is act out our little charade." She reached over and kissed him. "Like this," she said, enjoying the warm sensation. "He'll leave us alone—everybody knows lovebirds enjoy being alone—and we'll see what we're not supposed to see."

Zack sat back and was silent for a moment. "Promise me you'll be extra careful from now on. No solo acts."

"I can take care of myself."

"I know that. But I have to think of Kate's safety, too. You understand, don't you?"

Lilli nodded and admitted to herself that she hadn't thought of Kate. "Call Lobo and tell him about the orchid tattoo. And mention that the guy has an accent, not French or Spanish, but something debonair like that. And his clothes were expensive. He's good-looking, too. Did I already mention that?"

"I'll call Lobo," Zack said, pulling out his cell phone. "And then let's go see the spunky Timucua Maiden."

"I can hardly wait," Lilli said, feeling a twinge of jealousy.

SEVEN

The Legend of Tomokie

LILLI AND ZACK MINGLED with the crowd gathered around a large stage built over a pond. The energized audience munched snacks, sipped soda and listened to those hearty Floridians who returned with out-of-town guests eager for a taste of 'real Florida.' Lilli tried to enjoy their stories, but she couldn't shake her fear that danger lurked in Tomoka Park. Trouble could strike at any moment.

A shrill birdcall pierced the air. Startled, the crowd hushed and stared up at the tree closest to the pond. An actor, dressed as a Timucua brave, with white wings strapped to his shoulders, balanced on a high branch. Gripping a rope wrapped with vines, he pushed off, swung down and landed on the stage.

The crowd leaned forward, eager to hear the Tale of Tomokie. "I am a messenger sent from the Great Spirit," the birdman said, fluttering his feathers. "I bring the Water of Life to this spring. May the dew from my wings once again give the waters their special powers."

Switching from camera to binoculars, Lilli scanned the faces of the crowd from her vantage point, off to one side. She recognized Russell and several other bikers, but couldn't locate the man with the orchid tattoo.

A loud and steady tom-tom beat came from the far side of the pond where several braves knelt beside their drums. A muscular middle-aged actor, with a red cloak tossed over his shoulder, strode to the center of the bridge. His huge feathered headdress shook with his every step. "I am Chief Tomokie," he said, raising his chin toward the sky. "I obey no rules except my own. Ha!" he spat the word. "I shall drink of these sacred waters." He seized a shiny golden cup tucked inside his cloak and raised it over his head. "Ha! I shall drink from this sacred cup."

Lilli hugged Zack. "Don't look now, but a man with a video camera at the birdman's tree has me worried. He keeps fidgeting with the camera. If I look his way, he steps back under the branches."

Zack put his arms around Lilli's waist and drew her close. "He's pretending to film the actors," he whispered in her ear. "But we're his real targets."

"Are we going to give him PG- or R-rated footage?" Lilli snuggled against Zack, enjoying his sudden show of affection, even though she knew his cuddling allowed him to furtively study the guy. She made a show of pushing Zack away. She snapped the zoom lens on her camera and pretended to take photos of Zack while she stole a close-up look at the guy by the tree. "His resemblance to the orchid-tattoo guy is uncanny," she said. "They could be brothers. This guy has shorter hair and no tattoo, but the face is very similar. They're definitely related."

The birdman flapped his wings and glided across the stage. "Beware, Tomokie!" he called out. "You know that the golden cup must not be touched by human hands. Tomokie, leader of a band of rebels, you insult all fifteen tribes of the noble Timucua with your actions. You provoke war!"

At the mention of war, warriors burst onto the scene, shaking gourd rattles. One of them, his body adorned with painted designs, called out, "We must prepare for battle with Tomokie's evil rebels." Tossing aside their bows, arrows and hatchets, the warriors performed an intricately choreographed routine of hand-to-hand combat. Dazzling lifts, tosses and somersaults brought cheers from the audience.

Suddenly, blood-curdling war whoops broke through the rhythmic drumming. Tomokie's rebels, their blood-red feathers quivering above their angry faces, charged onto the stage. They leaped onto the backs of the virtuous braves, who struggled, spun around, tipped forward and backward, trying to dislodge the clinging attackers from their shoulders. Finally the good braves succeeded and the crowd went wild.

"Our filmmaker by the tree is biding his time," Lilli said. "What do you suppose he's waiting for?"

"Probably the chance to check out your gear and see if you're on the up-and-up. Memorize Kate's phone number," Zack said, repeating it several times. "The way you go traipsing off with your cameras, I can't keep track of you. Call Lobo if we get separated."

Lilli gripped the straps of her tote bag as the drumming slowed to a single steady beat. Fifteen chiefs, wearing plumed headdresses with raccoon tails trailing down their backs to the middle of their capes, marched triumphantly to the beat of the drums. Forming a semicircle, they raised their arms over their heads and clapped their hands once. The music stopped. In that moment of dramatic silence, the warriors shouldered their bows and aimed their arrows at Tomokie. Everyone froze in place, resembling statues in a wax museum.

Suddenly, a beautiful maiden with long dark hair pranced onto the stage, greeted by cheers and whistles. A woman wearing a Daytona Beach T-shirt leaned close to Lilli. "She was Miss Volusia County and before that, Ormond High's homecoming queen," the woman said. "She's making it as a singer now. Headed straight for Nashville. Let me tell you, she's as good as Faith Hill, and that's saying something. Too bad they hide her hair beneath that wig. Blond—"

"I am Oleeta," the maiden said. She was clothed only in Spanish moss artfully concealing her flesh-colored bikini. "And I seek justice for the Timucua."

"Go girl!" a woman cheered from the audience.

Oleeta nodded appreciatively. "Chief Tomokie a symbol of arrogance, must not live to see another sunrise!"

"Go get him, honey!" a man's voice rumbled.

Oleeta knelt down, dipping her fingertips into the pond and cameras clicked. She stirred the water, as if testing the temperature, and smiled at the cameras. Her well-toned body, coated with oil, glistened in the sunlight.

"Go Oleeta! Go Oleeta!" the crowd roared.

Oleeta bounded to her feet and shook off the drops of water. "Tomokie has defiled these waters. He must die!"

"Whoa, baby! Let him die a happy man," a male voice shouted.

Oleeta grabbed an arrow from the ground where one of the warriors had left it. Lilli could see it was made of cardboard. Oleeta rushed at Tomokie, and stabbed him in the chest. Gasping and writhing, he collapsed at her feet. Oleeta dragged his lifeless body to a tree stump and propped him up. "Justice has been served!" she shouted and seized the golden cup from his hand. He held onto it in a death grip and the crowd yelled, "Take it, Oleeta!"

"Alas!" exclaimed the birdman, who fluttered by. "While saving the golden cup from disgrace, Oleeta failed to see the danger in her midst."

Lilli snuggled closer to Zack, as if the words were directed at her.

"Tragedy has struck!" The birdman shook his head. "A poisoned arrow flew its deadly course straight to Oleeta."

Oleeta slumped to the floor, clutching the golden cup.

Rolling over and over, she tumbled from the stage into the pond and disappeared beneath the dark waters.

"Our guy is packing up his video camera," Zack warned. "He's ready to make his move."

War broke out again amongst the braves. This time, Tomokie's evil warriors were quickly defeated and fell in a heap on the stage. "And thus died Tomokie's rebels," the birdman intoned as the drums beat a dirge.

Lilli realized that Oleeta had been in the water all this time. Relieved, she saw the tip of a green plastic reed poking from the water and recognized an old trick from adventure movies. With sad face, the warriors lifted Oleeta's body from the spring and placed it on a stretcher made from a blanket and poles. They carried her slowly and reverently across the bridge and laid her to rest in a bed of ferns beside the pond. Peering through her binoculars, Lilli saw a warrior place a small microphone by Oleeta's hand. Lilli noticed several bare spots among the ferns and wondered if plants had been removed to protect them during the performance.

Bam! Bam! Bam! Explosions came from somewhere near the stage. Oleeta sat bolt upright. "What the heck was that?" she demanded from her graveside.

"Let's get out of here," Zack said, steering Lilli in the direction of their car.

Bam! Bam! Bam! More explosions. Plumes of foul smelling smoke clouded the air. In the confusion of people running and ducking for cover, the guy with the video camera charged toward Lilli and Zack. They struggled through the frightened crowd, looking for an opening to break away.

"Don't panic!" a deep voice bellowed. "It's only fireworks."

"There's the guy who set off the fireworks!" came another voice. "He ruined the show for us. Let's get him!"

Elbowing her way forward, Lilli heard a man cry out, "Stop him!"

Lilli turned and saw Russell tackle the guy with the video camera. "Get the ranger over here!" Russell shouted. The man leaped to his feet, leaving his video camera behind and ran. Zack chased after him, but lost him in the thick foliage that separated the river from parkland. Tote bag still clutched tightly in her hand, Lilli caught up to Zack. "Which way did he go?" she asked.

Zack kicked the ground. "He's disappeared into the bushes like a green ghost. But we may have a break. I saw the ranger pick up the video camera. We may get a good set of prints."

Gasping for breath, Russell stumbled toward Zack and leaned on his shoulder. "Trouble sure follows wherever you go, old buddy. It's a real shame. Now we won't get to hear Oleeta and her heavenly band of maidens sing the farewell lament. I've been waiting days for this. It's enough to make a grown man cry."

People wandered by, complaining that they had missed out on Oleeta's angelic voice. One woman mumbled, "That guy tried to hurt Oleeta. If we find him, he's in big trouble."

"Okay, everybody, settle down. Park Ranger Al Andrews, at your service," the ranger said, toting the video camera on his shoulder. "I promise you we'll get to the bottom of this." He adjusted the visor that kept his sandy blond hair out of his eyes. Lilli was already sizing him up in case of more trouble. He had a slight paunch, but was basically in good shape.

"Is Oleeta okay?" a man asked.

"She's shaken, but she'll be fine," Ranger Al said. "We apologize for the inconvenience. Now, I'd like to hear from anyone who can provide a description of the man." Details flew and Ranger Al recorded everything in his pocket notepad. "I'll turn over this information to the police. They're on their way."

"We'll stay out of this for now," Zack said to Lilli. "We need to get a handle on what's happening here."

The sudden roar of heavy-duty machinery came from the riverbank.

"Follow me. The show's not over, folks," Ranger Al shouted, backing himself toward the river. "We have a special treat today. Buzz saws are about to uncover the ancient secrets of the Timucua. Let's go!"

EIGHT

The Midden Mound

LILLI, ZACK AND THE CROWD gathered near the roped-off excavation area. They watched two workers midway up the eight-foot mound of soil who were busily sawing straight toward the bottom. Chunks of soil embedded with shell fragments tumbled to the ground. Other workers scooped them into wheelbarrows and transported them to a nearby building, where they would later be examined for artifacts. Lilli could see that the sawing process would eventually reveal a cross-section of the mound from top to bottom.

Ranger Al tapped his palm against his fingertips signaling 'time out.' The grateful crew turned off their machinery, tipped back their hard hats and guzzled bottled water. The pleasant sounds of the river's gurgling and birds' chirping returned once again to Tomoka Park.

"You are about to see the past come alive," Ranger Al said proudly. Lilli thought if his chest swelled any more, he might pop his buttons. "This midden mound, a refuse pile of invaluable cultural artifacts, will offer clues to the Timucua diet and activities. After we complete the sawing and hauling, the mound's interior will be exposed from the highest point to the lowest. When that's done, we plan to install a transparent panel so that visitors can observe all levels."

Ranger Al's eyes turned steely with determination. "Let me point out that we are not being disrespectful to the memory of the Timucua. This is not a ceremonial mound and is in no way connected to burials. After careful consideration, we selected this particular midden for our living history display because visitors, thoughtless visitors, have already disturbed it. Some unsupervised digging has occurred, as you can see."

He pointed to several areas where the soil had been dug up and packed down. "History in the making…" He signaled the workers to resume their work. "History," he continued, but the buzz saws cut him off.

Changing cameras and film, Lilli's thoughts raced. Had visitors—or park personnel, as she'd assumed—dug up the fern bed where Oleeta was laid to rest? Or was it the work of someone with criminal motives? If so, what did they hope to find? Did the fern bed and the midden mound hold clues to Zack's investigation? The ferns lay at the pond's edge and the midden sat along the riverbank. Did water, possibly something near the water or in the water, hold the key that would unlock the puzzle?

A shrill scream pierced the steady drone of the buzz saw. Lilli turned to see a tourist pointing into the rubble. The workers cut their engines as others shouted. Lilli looked up and saw the burly worker drop his buzz saw and jump to the ground. He had a look of sheer terror on his face. "Ranger Al!" he shouted, as the other worker touched down next to him. "There's a body in the midden!"

Lilli caught up to Zack, who had already moved closer to the mound. A pant leg and boot poked out of the soil. For once Zack did not try to shield her.

"Photograph everything, Lilli," Zack ordered. He leaned over the excavation ropes for a closer look at the ghoulish discovery.

"Let's clear the area in an orderly manner," Ranger Al commanded. His voice wavered. It told Lilli dead bodies were not an everyday occurrence at this dig, especially fully clothed ones. "The police are already in the park investigating the firecracker and smoke-bomb incident. They've been alerted," Ranger Al said, waving his walkie-talkie. He shooed the children away. "There are plenty of other demonstrations. Visit the basket weavers. Enjoy the fresh-baked coontie-fern bread. Go on, now. You, too, sir," he said to Zack.

Lilli watched as Zack discreetly flashed his badge, shook hands, and spoke in a hushed voice with Ranger Al.

"On a day like this," Ranger Al said, slapping Zack on the back, "I can use all the help I can get." He continued herding the last of the straggling visitors away from the site as the police siren came near. "Try your luck at the yopantea spitting contest," he urged two lingering boys, who were about ten years old. "The Timucua brave who could keep down the sacred tea the longest and then vomit the furthest was man enough to go on warring parties." The boys raced off and the crowd was completely dispersed.

"I didn't let on why we're here," Zack confided to Lilli. "I offered to stay and help maintain order until the Ormond Beach officers arrive." He pulled out his cell phone and punched in numbers. "Lobo, it's Zack." He quickly explained everything that had happened. "Your fellow officers will be here any minute. I don't want to interfere, but I need to know the identity of the body in the midden mound as soon as possible. When you hear anything, anything at all, get back to me." While Zack listened, his face turned more serious with each passing second. "I'll give Lilli the secure numbers," he said finally and hung up.

"What's wrong?" Lilli asked.

"Lobo and Jones spotted a repairman on a telephone pole near Kate's condo. They checked. The phone company found an unauthorized tap on Kate's phone." He jotted down phone numbers on a slip of paper. "From now on, use Jones and Lobo's line for anything confidential."

In minutes, the site was swarming with Ormond Beach police who secured the site and then uncovered the body. Zack stayed out of their way, having learned from experience that locals don't appreciate sugges-tions from out-of-towners. "The guy's been dead about a week," a baby-faced officer said. He grimaced and gagged.

Zack leaned closer, but was still at a discreet distance. "Geez!" He coughed, covering his nose with his handkerchief. "Lilli, zoom in on the belt buckle before they remove the body, but don't be too obvious."

Lilli pulled up the bandana from her neck so that it masked her face. "Is there something special about the buckle?" she asked. She snapped several photos, pretending interest in a snow-white ibis that had just landed gracefully on its spindly legs.

"Could be. It reminds me of the belt buckle on the body in New York. Embossed silver with fancy stuff along the edges. This buckle may have an elephant's head in the middle. It's hard to make it out with all the debris. The one in New York had a monkey. I'll bet they're from the same craftsman."

"Zack, you're going to like this," Lilli said. "The guy with the tattoo who spoke to me? I noticed he had a silver ponytail clip. It was embossed and looked very expensive. I don't know if there was an animal's head on it, but it's possible."

Zack punched his fist against the palm of his hand. "You've got sharp eyes, Lilli. We're finally getting somewhere. Once we identify the body, we're on our way to cracking this case. There's got to be a connection to Benjamin Voda and the shoot-out rampage near here. Selling illegal firearms was my first hunch and I'm sticking with it. Voda kept a huge arsenal. It's stretching a clue, but elephants are still slaughtered for their tusks."

"In Florida?"

"This case may go beyond U.S. borders," Zack said. "Voda's illegal weapons came from far and wide."

"How does the monkey figure in?" Lilli asked.

Zack shrugged. "When we know that, we'll be one step closer to an arrest." He looked around. "There's nothing more we can do here. Is there anything we might have overlooked in the rest of the park?"

"We should take the canoe trip we talked about. I think water plays a role in whatever is going on in Tomoka Park. The midden is close to the river. Whoever buried the body might have come by boat."

"Good thinking. Ever thought of a career change?"

LILLI AND ZACK DROVE back to the launch area where a gangly teenager, with Boat Attendant printed on his T-shirt, leaned against a stack of life preservers. His name tag identified him as Todd.

"Whazzup?" Todd asked, working his way through a family-size bag of potato chips.

"We'd like to rent a boat," Zack said. "What do you recommend?"

Todd tapped the toe of his sneaker against one of the sleek sleigh-shaped boats tied to the dock. "Airboats are for speed freaks, thrill seekers. You know, younger guys." Zack flinched. Todd popped a handful of chips in his mouth and pointed at the pontoon boats. "Slow and steady, but they're reserved for large groups." He walked along the dock and tapped the toe of his other sneaker against a kayak. "Not for beginners. They tip easily. Lose your boat, lose your deposit. No exceptions." He pointed at a small canoe and shrugged.

"I can tell the canoe is low on your totem pole," Zack said, pausing for a laugh that never came, "but if it was good enough for Timucua, it's good enough for us."

"Whatever, man." Todd sighed loudly as if he'd heard Zack's comments a million times before.

Zack paid the rental fee and deposit with his credit card. He slipped the boy a folded bill and pointed toward the parking area. "Make sure nobody messes with our car. It's the silver Taurus."

Todd sniffed. "Looks like somebody already got to your window."

Zack turned to Lilli and muttered, "Whazzup?"

"Whatever, man," she muttered back.

Lilli's stomach growled. "Sounds like I've worked up an appetite for whatever Kate packed in our picnic cooler."

"Bad thinking." Zack shook his head. "You've never sampled one of Kate's picnics. But we'd better eat before setting out on the river."

While Zack unloaded the picnic cooler at a shady table, Lilli selected a disposable camera from her tote bag. She locked her good cameras and film in the car trunk and sat down opposite Zack, who was unwrapping two wheat buns. He lifted the top of his and peered cautiously at the contents as if a tarantula were waiting to strike. "Hot dog!" he exclaimed.

"I would have expected something vegetarian," Lilli commented.

"You'll regret that remark," Zack said. "It's Kate's triple threat: grilled tofu, marinated eggplant and roasted peppers. And we can wash it all down with—" he studied the canned drink "—a strawberry and alfalfa shake."

"Here's to your good health," Lilli said, clicking her shake against his. "At the bikers' camp I'm sure we'll see very different culinary choices."

Zack smacked his lips. "Barbecued ribs, baked potatoes dripping with sour cream and real butter, beans swimming in fried onions and bacon bits, gallons of cold beer. Oh yeah, I'm ready for a hearty dose of cholesterol. Clog my arteries! See if I care!"

Lilli enjoyed Zack's playful streak and nearly forgot they were at Tomoka Park on police business. But every now and then, if a twig snapped or an unexpected sound came from the woods or water, she saw Zack's professional instincts kick in. Detective Zack Faraday's jaw tightened, his muscles flexed and his unblinking eyes surveyed the bushes and coquina rocks searching for dangers that might lurk there.

"We'd better get going," Lilli said, checking the sky. She hated to end their pleasant lunch break, but a cluster of smoky gray clouds passed over. The water that had been an inviting sunlit blue now appeared murky, its surface ruffled.

NINE

The Canoe Trip

LILLI AND ZACK STRUGGLED to adjust their bulky life
vests and steady their canoe while they synchronized
their paddle strokes. After a while, like old pros, they
managed to relax and paddle at a comfortable pace.
They waved to the few boaters that passed and seemed
to be heading in. Occasionally they stopped to examine
through their binoculars anything that attracted their
attention. They were looking for something, but they
didn't know what. Zack assured her they would know
what when they spotted it.

"I wish I'd brought my zoom lens," Lilli said, nodding toward a grove of cypress leaning over the water's
edge. "What a great shot—a lone fisherman squatting
on the far riverbank fishing with a bamboo pole."

"It's an old southern tradition," Zack said. "A man, a
cane pole, a straw hat and a can of worms." He chuckled.
"These backwater haunts are where you'll find the true
freshwater fisherman. If you want a good story, ask
Kate about last July when she dragged me to Dusty's
Last Stand Fish Camp. Kate wanted some sketches for

her Old Florida series. Dusty, a friend's uncle and an ardent fan of her work, was glad to oblige."

"I'm a captive audience right now. Why don't you tell me yourself," Lilli said over her shoulder.

Zack slowed his paddling. "Kate parked the van about an hour from here, honked the horn, and Dusty—hip boots, raggedy clothes, bushy beard and all—stomped out of the bushes like some horror movie swamp thing. We carted Kate and all her paraphernalia to his place. It was a combination bait shack, supply store and souvenir shop, connected to his bar and grill. It looked like a wood pile ready to collapse, rickety docks and all."

"I can't picture Kate in such rustic surroundings," Lilli said.

"Kate loved it. While she sketched, I played poker and drank beer with Dusty's cronies. Picture us surrounded by gator key chains, gator mugs, stuffed gator heads and two stuffed gators as big as trucks. I was losing my shirt, my brand new gator T-shirt, when the sputtering of a pontoon boat told us we had visitors."

Lilli halted her stroke and turned toward Zack.

"Keep paddling and keep a sharp lookout," Zack reminded her,

"Okay, but tell the rest of the story."

"Would you believe a dozen retired seamstresses from Duluth, sporting name tags on matching blouses? Their group leader, I think her name tag said Doris, explained they were headed to Captain Ed's Riverboat Canteen, part of their Real Florida Excursions tour. But when the river split, they chose the wrong stream and were then completely lost."

Zack laughed heartily. "'Would it be possible,' Doris asked, flashing some bills, 'to substitute Dusty's Fish Camp for Captain Ed's Riverboat?' Dusty, a man who appreciates the unexpected, agreed. He barked orders at his cronies, his 'wait staff,' and me, his 'maitre d',' and in no time, 'the Duluth dozen,' as Dusty called the ladies, were happily devouring frogs, which he called 'Creole hopping fish,' catfish and gator, which Dusty labeled 'Low Country chicken.'"

Zack laughed again. "Here comes the best part. They paid Kate for five-minute caricatures. They assumed that Kate, sitting in the shade with her sketchpad, was on call for tourists. Doris assured Kate that she could make a good living on Duluth's flea market circuit. I hadn't seen Kate laugh like that in years. Between caricatures, she nibbled saltines and claimed they were genuine Florida crackers."

Lilli had never loved Zack more than at this very moment. He was a man's man at home in the world of fish camps, but when his sister was involved, his gentle protective side showed up. Lilli wished that Zack felt as much affection for her as for his sister. Wasn't this crazy? Was she jealous of Kate? Crazier yet, was Kate jealous of her?

Before Lilli could answer her own questions, a bee flew inside her collar. She slapped at her neck and squirmed like a kid in an over-starched shirt.

"What's wrong?" Zack asked.

"A bee!" Lilli exclaimed and yanked off her life jacket.

A flock of dark birds shot across the surface of the river as if disturbed by something or someone. "Head for shore," Zack prompted, his voice sharp with urgency. Their canoe lunged forward as his paddle sliced through the water. Lilli paddled as fast as she could.

A sudden roar, as loud as an aircraft engine, blasted from somewhere behind. Lilli turned and saw an airboat zooming over the water like a hydroplane. It barreled toward them. Lilli caught a glimpse of the driver wearing a wet suit and goggles. He was too short and stocky to be the orchid tattoo man or his look-alike relative. Terror gripped Lilli. She screamed, hoping against all hope that the driver would turn away in time. She prayed that she and Zack would survive.

The airboat bounced hard on the water. Wave after wave battered the tiny canoe. Lilli's life jacket flew from her lap. Her paddle fell into the water. The canoe rocked side to side, and then flipped over. Down, down Lilli sank into the murky waters, her boots as heavy as cement shoes. Fear turned to panic. She couldn't see. Her ears pounded. She floundered, struggled toward the surface. But was it the surface? She couldn't tell up from down. Her lungs felt as if they would burst. Sputtering, gulping air, Lilli finally broke through the surface.

Treading water, she struggled to push her hair out of her eyes and get her bearings. Blinking away muddy water, she saw the grassy riverbank pounded by waves from the airboat. Two black tires wriggled from the grass, rolled into the water and disappeared beneath the roiled surface. Hold on! One of the tires partially surfaced and glided through the ripples. Good God! Was her mind playing tricks? She saw a long snout. A short distance away, a tail swished. They weren't tires. They were alligators!

Where was Zack? Lilli panicked. Where was Zack? She saw the airboat circling, whipping up more waves, racing back for another hit. The noise was deafening. Suddenly she felt Zack grabbing her by the waist. He pulled her in his strong grip toward shore.

"Gators!" she exclaimed. "Coming this way!" She broke free, swimming fast and hard, matching him stroke for stroke, despite her heavy boots.

Lilli heard the crash as the airboat plowed into their abandoned canoe. When she looked back, the split canoe was flying into the darkening sky and the airboat was racing back toward the launching area. An adrenaline rush pushed her onward. She swallowed water, but kept on swimming, kicking and stroking faster than she had ever moved in her entire life. Her heart raced. The pounding in her head grew louder, like Timucua drums during battle.

Lilli and Zack dragged themselves into the reeds and scrambled up the riverbank. "The alligators?" Lilli cried.

"Gone. The waves must have confused them," Zack said between rasping breaths.

Exhausted and shaking from their ordeal, Lilli and Zack rested on dry land. "We've got to get back to the launch area," Zack finally said, pulling her to her feet. "Have you got your wind back?"

Lilli nodded, fighting off the terror of what might have happened. Water sloshed from her boots as she stumbled through ferns and fallen cypress needles, dodging moss-covered logs. She let go of Zack's hand to slap away the no-see-um bugs that flew up her nose and stuck to her neck. Guttural croaking sounds came from somewhere nearby, and Lilli envisioned a swamp creature, half man half beast, lunging toward her. More croaking sounds erupted and Lilli imagined two gigantic gators, jaws open, teeth chomping, charging after her.

"Frogs," Zack said, catching his breath and nodding at the shiny bulging-eyed creatures hopping from log to log.

Lilli laughed at her own foolishness. Then her laughter turned to anger. "He tried to kill us!" she exclaimed.

"No. If he'd wanted to kill us, he could have. He only wanted to give us a good scare."

"Well, that's a comfort!"

"Somebody wants us out of here," Zack said. "Something's about to go down in Tomoka Park and they don't want us around when it does."

"Well, he's not scaring me away. I have a dinner

date tonight with the bikers and I wouldn't miss it for anything."

"You are one very feisty woman! Has anybody ever told you that before?"

She laughed, picking a mud-caked tendril off her forehead. "Yes. On several occasions."

Zack put his arm around her and led her toward the main trail. "Let's see what Todd can tell us about the guy who rented the airboat. And then I think we've earned a hot shower at Kate's. What do you say?"

"I think we're going to get nature's own shower," she said, peering at the rain clouds gathered above the treetops. "Those drums I thought I heard are thunder." She turned for one last look at the river. She shivered in the cool breeze. Lightning zigzagged across the blackening sky.

"Run!" Zack shouted.

Lilli and Zack ran toward the main trail. Could they be running into an unknown and unstoppable enemy?

TEN

Good Cop, Bad Cop

LILLI AND ZACK THANKED the park workers for the ride and hopped off the tram. "At least our car's still in one piece," Lilli said, wiping the raindrops from her face.

Zack unlocked the trunk and pulled his wallet from his gym bag. "And it looks like nothing was disturbed. I want to talk to our teenaged friend Todd again."

"Are you going to pay him for information?" Lilli asked as Zack stuffed bills in his pockets.

"You saw his entrepreneurial eyes light up when I tipped him. Let's see what he can add to our description of the guy in the airboat." Water sloshing from his sneakers, Zack stormed toward the boat rental shack.

"Is this where you play bad cop and I'm the good cop?" Lilli asked, hurrying to keep up.

"That's TV theatrics," Zack said, but Lilli was already practicing her sweetest smile.

"Whazzup?" Todd asked as he squashed an empty bag of cheese doodles.

"Let's cut to the chase," Zack growled. "I want to know how the guy who rented the airboat got here, how he paid, where he went when he left here and anything else you can think of, including a description. And I don't want to hear vague crap like 'whatever.'" Zack spat the words, mere inches from Todd's face.

"Something green would rev up my memory and my vocabulary," Todd said with a sly grin, and Zack thrust a wad of bills at his outstretched hand.

"The guy you're looking for came on foot," Todd said, fanning the bills and then pocketing them. "He's stock and real surly. He walked up to me wearing a wet suit, goggles and a bandana over his head, so I didn't get a real good look at his face. He jammed a lot of money in my hand—a whole lot more than you're showing me—and chose an airboat. Off he went. A kayaker paddled back and told me what happened. Too bad, man. I didn't know he planned to swamp your canoe. What am I, a mind reader? Here." He counted out two bills and handed them to Zack. "Have a cup of coffee on me."

Fuming, Zack pushed aside the bills. "Where did he go after he returned the airboat?"

"I'm not sure."

"Think hard," Zack said, his eyes squinting with anger.

"Hey, I'm thinking, but nothing's coming through." Todd tapped his pocket, and Zack stuffed in more bills. "It's crystal clear now," Todd said. "I'd say he's a biker. He's probably staying in the skuzzy part of biker camp."

"What clued you in?"

"The spiked dog collar around his neck."

Lilli leaned into the conversation and flashed a bill along with her sweetest smile. "I can't afford full sentences," she said, "so please nod if you agree. Do we have a deal?"

He nodded.

"Was the guy shorter than you?"

Nod.

"Stockier?"

Nod.

"Brawnier?"

Nod.

"Smarter?"

Shrug.

"Possibly a weight lifter?"

Nod.

"Mustache?"

Nod.

"Dark mustache?"

Nod.

"Making as much money as you are?"

Shrug and grin.

Zack nudged Lilli. "Let's go before Todd finds his thesaurus and we blow all our money."

Todd ripped open a bag of corn chips. "Before you take your good-cop bad-cop show on the road, I should remind you…" he chomped a mouthful of chips "…no canoe, no deposit return, no exceptions."

Zack stormed away, muttering, "He thinks he's had the last word."

"He has." Lilli laughed. "Come on, Zack. Save your anger for the guy with the dog collar."

"That can wait until we talk to Billy Bob. He doesn't miss much. I bet he'll know the guy and point him out. If I'm right, then once it's dark, I'll see what I can find in that creep's trailer or tent...or doghouse." Zack sneered. "It's going to be one hell of an evening at biker camp when I pry his collar off with a crowbar."

"We're going to biker heaven, not hell, remember? Now let's get out of these wet clothes and into something more suitable for a good cop and bad cop."

ELEVEN

Bud's Blooms

"ZACK, HOW DO YOU FEEL about coincidences?" Lilli asked cheerfully as they drove away from Tomoka Park. She was feeling much better in dry clothes.

"Romantically speaking?"

"Professionally speaking," Lilli said, and regretted cutting him off before he'd revealed his feelings.

"During a crime investigation, coincidences are red flags," Zack said.

"I thought so. Well, I noticed that the florist shop in town advertised an exotic plant show for this afternoon. Orchids are exotic. The guy who broke into our car and stole your notebook had an orchid tattoo on his arm. An interesting coincidence, would you say?"

"You are truly an incredible woman," Zack said and floored the gas pedal. "We'll swing by the florist's on our way to Kate's."

"I'VE NEVER SEEN SO MANY cars in the downtown area," Zack commented. "I wonder what's going on?" They finally found a parking place and hurried to Bud's Blooms. A security guard wearing an orchid pinned to his pocket stepped across their path, barring their entry. "I'll have to inspect your bag, ma'am," he said. "And I'll have to ask your bodyguard to submit to a quick frisk."

"Is there a problem?" Lilli asked. She noticed the proud look on Zack's face as he mouthed the word 'bodyguard,' and flexed his biceps.

"The usual problem," the guard said, poking through Lilli's camera supplies. "This orchid show is a pipsqueak compared to the big ones in Miami, but the competition is stiff and the prestige of winning is great. So who knows what harm could come to the precious flowers and their owners?"

"Harm?" Lilli commented.

The guard wagged his finger. "Don't ever underestimate flower power."

Lilli and Zack entered the shop, where several customers were looking at floral arrangements in baskets. The teenage clerk behind the cash register leaned forward. "Did you want to see something here in the showroom or are you here for the meeting?"

"The meeting," Lilli said and showed her camera. "I'm here to take photos. May I take one of you?"

"Of course," the clerk said, obviously flattered. She smoothed her lavender hair, anchored behind her ears by lavender blossoms that matched her lavender lipstick.

When Lilli had finished, the clerk pointed toward the rear. "The Ormond Orchid Society is hosting this meeting in our garden room," she said. "Next week, the Violet Society will take their turn, so I'll get double duty out of all this." She batted her lavender eyelids and wiggled her fingers, showing off sparkling lavender nails.

"You are a very colorful person," Lilli said admiringly.

"Most people aren't so complimentary," she said. "But you should see me during our annual spring flowers festival when I go for my rainbow effect." She leaned closer and confided to Lilli, "Uncle Bud, the owner, pays me extra to dress like this. He says it brings in the customers, but he's wasting his money. Orchid people don't need gimmicks. They're a crazy breed, if you get my meaning."

"Fanatics," Lilli said. "Capable of anything. Theft, assault...murder."

"I can tell this isn't your first orchid show."

Lilli followed the signs to the garden room, weaving through tables filled with brochures and orchid culture displays. "This is a world I never knew existed," Lilli said, perusing the services offered to orchid lovers. "Can you imagine? Orchid doctors who promise to nip life-threatening maladies in the bud. Portraitists who will paint your orchid family. Architects who specialize in unique habitats for orchids." She chuckled. "Imagine this...music to soothe restless orchids."

"Would you believe visiting care-givers for orchids?" Zack quoted from his brochure: "Let our experts nurture your plants while you're on vacation." He whistled through his teeth. "Orchid investors' clubs are big business. The international trade in orchids accounts for more than fifteen billion dollars annually."

"This beats all," Lilli said, reading a brochure's bold print. "Would you wish to be seen naked by strangers? Of course not. Then why embarrass your orchids in their undressed stage? Let one of our orchid boarding establishments house the shy darlings until they produce buds and are ready to be seen by your guests."

"I can't wait to hear what they're discussing in there," Zack said. He opened the grilled gate and stepped into the garden room, a shady courtyard enclosed by walls of banana trees, nestled beneath shady oaks. Huge blowers hissed warm moist air across the two hundred or so people perched on folding chairs. Many cradled their orchids near their hearts and caressed their orchids' ribbons that boasted First, Second and Third place.

Lilli regretted that she and Zack had missed the judging. She hoped the guest speakers flanking the podium would prove interesting.

"I bring news from the orchid-breeding world," the speaker in the dark suit was saying. "For years, I have cross-pollinated my favorites from the sixty thousand known orchid species, hoping to produce a unique beauty. I was this close to my life's ambition." His thumb and index finger indicated an inch. "But my brand of creation is passé. Orchid cloning..." he shook his head sadly "...is blossoming."

Moans of regret rose from the audience.

"Orchid laboratories are replacing greenhouses."

Another wave of moans rippled across the room.

"And so, I regretfully say 'farewell.' I hope you will gather the courage to banish those…" his voice cracked "…those despicable cloners from our midst. Use whatever methods—brutal, even barbarian—you deem necessary."

A loud volley of applause followed him to his seat.

"Brutal? Barbarian?" Lilli whispered to Zack. "We've stumbled onto something nasty, that's for sure."

The next speaker was already slamming his fist on the podium. "I must address the most horrid of crimes—flowernapping! Last month the rare ghost orchid was taken from its secure place behind shatterproof glass in Atlanta's Flower Museum. The surveillance cameras mysteriously—Ha!—blacked out during a suspicious—Ha!—power outage. Just yesterday, that rare one-day bloomer, the Stanhopea, was flowernapped en route to New Orleans. Am I at liberty to exhibit my delicate lady's-slipper today? No! And why not? Because it too has been flowernapped and probably sold to an unscrupulous collector. The going rate is an unbelievable thirty thousand dollars! The sad truth is that crime, motivated by greed, is strangling botany."

All this talk about flowernapping made Lilli think about the missing ferns near Oleeta's graveside at Tomoka Park. Was there some connection between orchids and ferns?

Bud, the owner of Bud's Blooms, a tall man with a shock of dark hair and gaunt face, strode to the podium.

"I've been asked to share a few words of wisdom," he said solemnly and adjusted his glasses. "The orchid, with a well-deserved reputation for being a most prolific, beloved and extraordinary plant, offers us many lessons. Orchids have learned to thrive in inhospitable domains, even in treetops, where they soar above all others. And so, let us strive to be like them and rise above all petty concerns." He rocked back on his heels, obviously overwhelmed by the power of his words. "Are there any questions before we close our meeting?"

Lilli's hand shot up.

Zack whispered, "What are you doing?"

"Getting answers," Lilli whispered back.

"The woman in the back," Bud said, pointing directly at Lilli.

"Do flowernappers ever take ferns?"

Several hisses and 'boos' stung Lilli's ears.

Bud's face turned bright red. He held his hands up and the crowd hushed. "Young lady, you have the nerve to come to an orchid meeting and mention ferns? Would you go to a vegetarian meeting and mention steak? Ferns, for land's sakes!"

"Sorry," Lilli murmured, thankful that at least he had referred to her as a 'young' lady. "The beauty of so many orchids all in once place must have driven me temporarily insane." She worked her way past hostile faces and menacing eyes.

Zack followed at her heels. "Let's get out of here," he urged, "before they spray us with pesticides!"

"Whew!" Lilli said as she and Zack escaped to the near-empty showroom.

"A rough meeting?" the clerk asked.

Lilli nodded and headed to the front door.

Zack confided to Lilli, "I never knew flowers could stir such passion."

"Didn't you go to your senior prom?"

Zack ignored her question. "What I'm saying is maybe plants, not guns, are behind the murders in New York City and Ormond Beach."

"After what I've seen here, I'd say it's possible."

"I didn't see any orchid tattoos in the audience," Zack said, "but I think orchids could have something to do with the Tomoka Park murder."

"I did see a few wild orchids in the park, but not the rare ones we heard about in Bud's Blooms." Lilli noticed a man and a woman marching back and forth in front of the shop carrying petitions. "Who are they?" Lilli asked the clerk.

"Crazy ex-orchid junkies. They're trying to hurt Uncle Bud's business."

"Why?" Lilli asked.

The clerk sniffed. "They overdosed on orchids and now they want to ban all orchid meetings."

Lilli stepped outside, holding her camera.

The woman rushed up to her. "Are you from the press? I've got to get my story out to the people who don't know that orchid mania can ruin their lives."

"That sounds a bit exaggerated," Lilli commented.

The woman shook her head. "I borrowed money for a hothouse. My husband put his foot down when I spent more on orchid food than the meals that went on our table. I couldn't stop, so he left me."

As Lilli tried to leave, the man joined in. "Beware the lust for orchids. You lose your money, your family, all to buy one more orchid." He waved his petition at Zack. "There was a time when I converted both my garages to greenhouses and filled them with orchids. Orchids were my passion, but now I'm on the road to recovery. Then along comes this orchid meeting and I feel myself slipping back. No more orchid shows!"

"Orchid passion takes over your life," chimed in the woman. "My friend wanted to see orchids in their natural habitat, so he liquidated his assets and set out for Asia. Now, his fortune is spent, and his homesick orchids are withering. No more orchid shows!"

Lilli saw Betty's pet store across the street and tugged at Zack's arm. "Let's go say 'hello' to Kate's friend Betty from the Up-Down league."

"Okay," Zack said. "But if her shop is anything like Bud's Blooms, we could be walking into a lion's lair."

Lilli laughed. "As they say, it's a jungle out there."

TWELVE

War of The Roses

BEFORE CROSSING THE STREET to Betty's pet shop, Zack phoned Lobo. "Busy," he said and waited for a line of cars to pass by. Somewhere in the distance, police sirens wailed.

"We can forget about seeing Betty," Lilli said, noticing the CLOSED sign on the door. "It appears she left in a hurry. Her bargain table is still sitting in front of her shop."

"Saved from the lion's lair after all," Zack said.

"I'm surprised Betty would close up early with so many people in town."

Zack smiled. "I've given up trying to figure out what women do and why they do it." He called Lobo again. "Still busy."

They had walked a few blocks back to their car when Zack held his hand to his ear as if to track the fading police sirens. "This certainly is a busy day for the Ormond Beach officers," Zack said and called Lobo again. "Lobo, it's Zack. Who've you been talking to for so long? Your bookie?" he joked. Then Zack's face paled, his smile disappeared and Lilli saw his serious professional expression take over. He listened intently to Lobo for several minutes. "I don't believe it," he said through gritted teeth and Lilli grew anxious as to what they were talking about.

After a long pause Zack repeated, "I don't believe it," and his voice seethed with anger. "How did they know Oliver and Betty were in Kate's tennis league?" he shouted into the phone. Grabbing hold of Lilli's hand, he started running toward the car. "Kate. Is Kate okay?" Zack shouted at Lobo and a chill ran up Lilli's spine. Another pause. Zack let go of Lilli's hand and kicked a discarded soda can down the sidewalk. "My God, poor Oliver," he said and fumbled for his car keys. "We're on our way."

"What happened?" Lilli asked as Zack pulled into traffic.

"Kate's tennis buddies have been hurt or scared out of their wits or both."

"Start at the beginning. Tell me everything Lobo told you."

Leaving the downtown traffic, Zack sped toward The Trails. "Kate's tennis buddy, Ike, called to tell her he'd been attacked in his apartment. A delivery person rang the doorbell and said he had a bouquet of roses from somebody named Kate in the Up-Down league."

Zack changed lanes and picked up speed. "When Ike opened the door, the delivery man barged in and roughed him up. Ike picked up his tennis racket and whacked the guy, knocking him down, leaving him dazed. Ike got out of there and wheeled himself to a neighbor's for help."

"How horrible!" Lilli exclaimed.

"Kate got real upset and Lobo grabbed the phone. Ike repeated everything to Lobo and Lobo sent an officer over right away. When Ike mentioned that the messenger claimed that Kate had sent the roses and that she was a member of the Up-Down league, Lobo knew that Kate's friends were in danger. He called Betty and Oliver and told them about Ike, and warned them to be careful."

Zack slammed on the brakes at the red light. "Unfortunately, the punk fled Ike's apartment before the police arrived. Luckily for us, he had let slip the name 'Up-Down league.' So we knew who he intended to hurt."

"My God!" Lilli exclaimed. "Was Betty attacked too? Is that why her shop was closed so hastily?"

"Lobo called Betty, explained everything and told her to leave her shop immediately." Zack roared into The Trails. "As she was locking up, she saw a delivery man with a bouquet of roses heading her way. She ran out the back door and didn't stop until she got to the police station."

"And Oliver?"

"Oliver wasn't so lucky. When Oliver didn't answer Lobo's call, Detective Jones raced over there—Oliver lives only two miles from Kate—and found him on the floor with a gash on his forehead. Jones took him to the emergency room."

Zack slammed on the brakes in Kate's driveway. He was out of the car and racing up the front path before Lilli had unfastened her seat belt.

"Calm down," Lobo greeted Zack. "Everything's under control. Nobody got near Kate. Oliver was released from the hospital. Ormond Beach's finest saw to it that Oliver, Betty and Ike are saying with friends and that no one followed them."

"Kate, are you all right?" Zack sputtered. He rushed to her side.

"I'm fine," Kate said, her face pale and drawn. "But my friends are a mess."

Zack growled, "When I get my hands on—"

"Take it easy," Lobo said and patted Zack on the shoulder. "Detective Jones is checking on Oliver, Betty and Ike. He's filing the paperwork and getting descriptions of the deliverymen. There were two, possibly three men involved. It was a well-coordinated effort."

"Cowards," Zack muttered, "picking on—"

"Cool it, Zack," Lobo said. "It's under control. Everyone's fine."

"Fine? You call this fine?" Mrs. D'Amato fumed from the living-room couch. "We're like birds in a gilded cage. We can't go anywhere until this War of the Roses is finished and everything returns to normal."

Kate wheeled herself across the living room. "Mrs. D'Amato, you have a short memory. Nothing has been normal around here since that maniac Voda went on a killing spree."

"This is all my fault," Zack said, putting his hand on Kate's shoulder. "If I'd stayed in a motel, no one would have connected you or your tennis friends to me."

"You can't be sure of that," Lilli said.

"Lilli's right," Lobo said. "These guys are obviously pros. They can find out whatever they want. This could have turned out badly, but it didn't. Let's try to figure out exactly what's going on here. The delivery stunt was obviously a diversionary tactic, a divide and conquer plan to scatter the Ormond Police officers around the city."

"To keep them away from whatever is about to happen in Tomoka Park or Ormond Beach," Zack said.

"Their message is clear," Lilli chimed in. "They could have hurt other people, but they chose the Up-Down league. Why? I think it's because they want you to stay here, Zack. They're afraid you might see something in Tomoka Park related to the New York murder. Something that could possibly escape the notice of local officers. They want you so worried about Kate that you'll stay here and watch over her instead of investigating the Tomoka Park murder. Or any other criminal activity in this area." She saw Kate's pained expression and immediately regretted her inference that Kate was a burden.

"Let me say what's on everyone's mind." Kate's cheeks were flushed with anger. "Those thugs think that because I'm in a wheelchair I'm weak and defenseless, but that's not so. Sure, I welcome police protection if my life is in danger. But I don't need or expect any more than Oliver or Betty or anybody else would receive." She held up her hand to ward off objections from Zack and Lobo. "And in case no one noticed, Ike did a fine job of defending himself from his wheelchair and escaping."

Lilli stammered, "Kate, I'm sorry. I hope you don't think—"

"My little speech wasn't directed at you, Lilli," Kate said. "And Zack and Lobo, I hope I don't sound ungrateful for your help. It's just that every so often, my anger boils over and I need to remind everyone, including myself, that I'm not incapacitated. Sorry." She wheeled off into the kitchen.

"She'll be fine," Zack said, stopping Lilli as she started after Kate. "She prefers to be alone at times like this, not the center of attention. She'll be her old cheerful self in no time."

Lobo cleared his throat. "The Ormond officers are still reeling from Voda's rampage. Let's get back to business and focus on what we can do to end this trouble as quickly as possible."

"I want the same thing you do," Zack assured Lobo.

"When there's a problem, I say 'eat!'" Kate set a tray of hors d'oeuvres on the coffee table next to the wine carafe. She smiled and any tension still remaining in the room disappeared.

"In Italy, we say *'buon appetito,'*" Mrs. D'Amato added, pouring herself a glass of wine. "But, of course, we say that when we are about to dive into a plate of pasta, not seaweed."

While Kate busied herself whirling more seaweed in the blender, Lobo confided to Zack, "I didn't want Ike, Betty or Oliver here. That's why I sent them to stay with friends. If anything goes down, the fewer people the better. Kate's a very capable woman, but 'No Unnecessary Risks,' that's my motto."

"Thanks." Appreciation shone in Zack's eyes. "I owe you one."

"Let's share what we know about Tomoko Park," Lobo said, taking charge.

"You first," Zack said.

Lobo separated the slats of the blinds and peered outside. "The body in Tomoka Park has a name. Ronny Miller. He's a penny-ante middle-man who cuts deals and brings people together."

"Looks like the people didn't like something Miller said or did," Zack said.

Lobo nodded. "From the defensive wounds on Miller's hands, we know he put up a good fight. He was outnumbered, judging from the sixteen stab wounds from three different blades."

Lilli flinched and dropped the cracker she was nibbling. "Do you think they dumped Miller in Tomoka Park because that's where they were conducting business? Or did they kill him elsewhere and move him?"

"Lilli's beginning to sound like a detective," Zack said.

"You should hear my wife." Lobo rolled his eyes. "She fires off questions like a woodpecker hammering at a tree trunk full of ants. Her questions steer me in new directions, and that stirs up answers. Then she gets on the phone and brags to her sisters how she cracked the case."

"At least your wife knows what you're doing," Zack said. "Lots of guys in my precinct complain that their wives tuned them out after they walked down the aisle."

Lobo waved away Zack's comments. "That's the way some wives handle stress. After Voda's rampage, most of us in the department elected to go through counseling with our spouses. I thought being a cop was tough work. I found out that being a cop's wife or a cop's husband is harder." He looked at Lilli. "The same is true, of course, for someone romantically involved with a cop. Life is fragile. One minute you're walking around and the next…" He sucked in his breath. "Sorry, Kate, I didn't mean—"

"It's okay." Kate set down another tray of hors d'oeuvres. "And you're right. Life is fragile, and not just for cops and their families. In any family, the lives of everyone hang from a single fragile thread. I once saw a drawing in a psychology book that has stuck with me for years."

"This isn't a good time for psychological discussions," Zack said forcefully and Lilli figured that Kate had struck a nerve.

Kate plowed on. "The father was at the top clutching a thread. Beneath him, the mother grasped the same thread, followed by the children from oldest to youngest, each with their fists balled up, holding on tight." Kate leveled her steady gaze at Zack. "Sometimes a family disagreement weakens the thread and no one dares to breathe, for fear the thread will break and the family collapse. Speaking as the eldest child, the child closest to the top, with the longest drop and hardest fall, I wouldn't choose to break the thread."

Lobo cleared his throat and looked from Kate to Zack and back to Kate again as if he had stepped into the middle of a family feud.

"The youngest, being closest to the bottom, escapes with the least harm. Is that your theory of the day?" Zack asked.

"It's more complicated than that. The youngest has a lot to lose. He could easily be buried by the weight of everyone falling on top of him. He wouldn't want that. Don't you agree?"

Zack huffed, "I don't sit around thinking about drawings in books and family problems from the past."

"Apparently you do," Kate replied.

Lilli figured Kate was referring to Zack's talks with the police psychologist. She saw in Zack's stunned expression that he had begun the painful confrontation with Kate that the psychologist had predicted.

"Know it off, you two," Lobo exclaimed. "Every time someone's in protective custody, this crap starts. It's like cabin fever. It will pass. Meanwhile, don't say anything you'll regret. I don't have time to referee family squabbles."

Lilli's head was spinning from the suffocating emotion flying between Kate and Zack. Whatever disagreement had occurred in the past had now come raging into the present like a ravenous shark, ready to rip apart both brother and sister. Lilli wondered if her coming to Florida had been such a good idea after all. Zack needed time alone with Kate. She was in their way. At the first opportunity, after she got her photos of biker camp, she would head for home.

Lilli realized that her one-track mind had kicked in: business first, then pleasure. But what pleasure could she hope to find here? Zack had no time for her. And he would never make time for her until he had worked out this lingering problem with Kate. If she had any sense at all, she would help the process along. Step in, be the peacemaker, help Zack and Kate settle their differences. And then, she'd sit back, radiant and smiling in the Florida sunshine, and watch Zack fall victim to her charm, good looks, intelligence and peacemaking skills.

Good. She had a plan. It wasn't a plan that had ever worked in the past. Okay, so maybe she was overrating her charm, good looks, intelligence and especially her peacemaking skills. Whenever she tried to help friends settle arguments, they made up and then had the nerve to turn against her. How many times had she told herself,

"Mind your own business. If they want advice, they'll ask for it."

Okay, now she had a plan. A good workable plan. Stay clear of Zack and Kate. Give them space to work things out. And then sit back, smiling and radiant in the Florida sunshine and watch him fall victim to her charm, good looks, intelligence and cool objectivity. She couldn't go wrong. No way!

As Lilli cleared her head, Lobo was saying, "Let's get back to the business at hand. We're checking on the dead man Ronny Miller and his known associates. That's a polite term for his buddies that hang out at Bottoms Up, a cheap dive over on Third Street. Miller didn't have the brain power to mastermind whatever's going on, so that brings us to the other suspects—the guy who came after you in the airboat, the guy with the orchid tattoo, his look-alike and the two or three men knocking on doors trying to deliver roses."

Zack popped a seaweed treat in his mouth. "Lilli and I found out from Billy Bob, a biker from heaven, so to speak, that the airboat guy is also a biker and he's staying at biker camp. Before we thank him for our pleasant little swim with the gators, I'd like to look around his place and see what turns up."

"Be careful," Lobo said. "We could send some men with you."

Zack shook his head. "We'll be okay. Some bikers we met will back me up."

"Lilli will stay here," Lobo said. "We agree on that, don't we, Zack?"

"Well I don't," Lilli said before Zack could speak. "I'm going with Zack."

"It's too dangerous," Lobo said.

"Zack will tell you, out in Grayrocks when the chips were down, I helped him out of a few scary situations. That was a lot more dangerous. This is just talking to a bunch of friendly bikers."

"She has a point," Zack added. "She could be helpful on this case. The bikers certainly want to do everything in their power to impress Lilli. She's doing an article on them for *Viewpoint* magazine."

Lobo narrowed his eyes. "She should stay here."

"No way!" Lilli exclaimed. "I'm going loaded with enough film to shoot every biker, bike, tent and trailer in sight."

"You won't talk her out of it," Zack said. "When Lilli sets her sights on something, you're a goner."

"I can see that," Lobo said and Lilli caught the knowing look he gave Zack. "But for the record, I'm opposed to Lilli going. She has no training in police work."

"You can't stop me," Lilli said.

Lobo sighed and threw up his hands in defeat. "As for the two guys who look alike," Lobo continued, "we got a match on the orchid tattoo. His name's Rick Santino, also known as Ricardo Santiago and Rich Sanders. My buddies are looking for him. He's been around the block, bounced back and forth between here, South America and Europe. He's a smooth operator who never gets his hands dirty. He carries the money from one place to another. And the lookalike, according to the prints on the video camera, is his cousin, Carl Santino."

"Let me guess," Mrs. D'Amato piped up. "His aliases are Carlos Santiago and Chuck Sanders."

"You're fast, Mrs. D'Amato," Lobo said admiringly.

"That comes from my years in the opera houses of Europe, where anything and everything can happen in a heartbeat." Mrs. D'Amato fluffed her scarf. "Orchids once played a nerve-wracking role during my performance at the Milan Opera House."

Zack said, "Maybe you could tell us later, Mrs. D'Amato, after—"

"The tenor was allergic to orchids." Mrs. D'Amato cut Zack off, rose to her feet, and burst into song. "Aahh! Aahh!" she punctuated the high notes with a scattering of 'Aahhs,' crinkling her nose and bobbing her head. "Each time I waited for the 'chooo!' as if I were expecting the other shoe to fall. Or should I say the other 'choo.'" She looked from one unsmiling face to the next. "If you don't mind my saying so, my orchid story is usually a big hit at parties, but I can tell you're not in the mood." She plunked herself down on the couch and sipped her wine.

"Actually I'm glad you brought up orchids," Zack said. "Lilli and I have a theory that plants, not guns, might be behind the trouble at Tomoka Park. Parks and maybe jungles are somehow involved. The dead body in New York had a monkey design on his belt buckle. The dead body in Tomoka Park had an elephant design. The guy with the orchid tattoo may have some kind of animal design on his ponytail holder. There's got to be a connection. And from what we saw at the orchid show today, murder stemming from flowers, pardon the pun, is very believable. Kate, do you mind if Lilli and I go check out some plants and animals on the internet before our rendezvous with the bikers?"

"I'll go with you," Kate said, wheeling herself into the elevator.

"Kate, you better stay downstairs with me," Lobo said. "I don't want you and Zack slugging it out up there and Lilli stuck as the referee."

"We can behave like civilized human beings," Kate snapped.

Lilli reluctantly climbed the stairs to the loft, wondering who would be the first casualty in Kate's civilized world.

THIRTEEN

Plants and Animals

LILLI ADMIRED THE GLEAMING wood banister as she
climbed the stairs to Kate's sitting area. Waiting for
Zack and Kate, who were riding up in the elevator, Lilli
looked over the railing at the foyer and the mosaic pattern of the bird in flight. She wondered how many times
Kate had looked at that bird and wished that she could
rise from her wheelchair and run with the wind.

"Please don't mind the mess," Kate said, steering
from the elevator to her computer alcove next to the sitting area. She nodded toward the tangle of fishing nets,
sponges and shells piled in the corner. "They're from a
recent trip to Tarpon Springs, a quaint village over on
Florida's west coast."

"Let me guess," Lilli said, constantly surprised by
Kate's active lifestyle. "When you're not painting or
playing tennis, you go fishing."

"That's true," Kate said. "But actually, I'm working on a collage up here where I have room to spread
out. Forget about the fishing stuff." Kate positioned her
wheelchair in front of her computer. "Wait until you

see my carpenter's ingenuity," she said, beaming with pride.

"You told me the carpenter had created a pull-out bookcase released by a lever," Zack said. "But I couldn't find it. I tried to show it to Lilli when we arrived."

"The lever's right there, third shelf from the bottom, camouflaged by the scroll trim. Just shift it to the left and presto! Magic."

"Very clever," Zack said and Lilli heard the sound of gears.

"Go ahead, Lilli," Kate said, "grab hold of any shelf and pull."

Lilli tugged and was amazed to see the bookcase slide forward on a metal track. Stepping behind the bookcase, she peered into the storage area and crawl space that led to air-conditioning ducts. "Wow! This is how I felt when I discovered my brother Pete's secret fort in the woods."

Zack laughed. "Your memories of the past are as sharp as Kate's."

Kate didn't prickle at Zack's comment and Lilli sensed that a temporary truce had been declared. Kate turned on the computer and logged onto the internet. "It's all yours, Lilli," she said, pushing herself away. "If you don't mind…" She picked up a stack of letters and magazines. "I'll hang around for a few minutes and sort through my mail." A quick glance revealed to Lilli that most of the correspondence was from galleries and museums.

"Lilli, while you're researching," Zack said, "I'm going to check out something by phone. I'll be in my bedroom if you come across anything interesting."

"What are you up to?" Lilli asked.

"I'm going to ask Digger, my friend at the precinct, to ferret out some information for us."

"What exactly are you looking for?"

"The passenger list for flights into Orlando, Miami, West Palm and Daytona, and any suspicious groups or known felons on board. Also, I'm going to call the big hotels in Ormond Beach and Daytona Beach, since both are near Tomoka Park. Let's see if any big events are scheduled or large blocks of rooms reserved. We could be missing the big picture of what's going on."

Kate looked up from an envelope she was tearing open. "You should call Betty, too. The Chamber of Commerce is closed for the day, but she's a member and she'll know if any special events are scheduled."

Lilli set to work. Soon she had a page of scribbled notes about orchids, ferns and plants to share with Zack in between his calls. "Plants are big business," she called out. "Twelve million orchids and eleven million cacti were sold last year on the international market. Now here's an interesting quote about the *illegal* market. 'The poaching of orchids and other plants from parks, jungles and forests is a global problem with tremendous ecological implications. Because of the lack of care in removing, transporting and nurturing plants, certain species face possible extinction.'"

"Give me some hard cold facts," Zack said, striding back to the computer alcove.

Lilli continued, "Last year, ginseng poaching in the Great Smokies brought five hundred dollars per pound. In Washington State, wholesalers in bark, moss, ferns and leaves grossed seventy thousand dollars a week. They use the stuff for herbal remedies and—for gosh sakes—floral arrangements."

"Like orchids maybe?"

"And roses for the Up-Down league?"

"You've got my interest," Kate said, peering around Lilli's shoulder and skimming the information on the screen. "Poachers in northwestern United States make a hundred bucks a night stealing and selling the exotic mushroom, matsutake. The chanterelle mushroom and the salad green, salal, are also sought after."

"Here's the criminal slant," Lilli said. "To avoid the expense of permits which allow daytime supervised harvesting, the poachers illegally enter parks and forests at night. Their crews are illegal immigrants, who can't risk being seen at a day job. Willing to work for next to nothing in order to send money home to their families, they are victimized by the poacher bosses who pocket most of the money."

Lilli turned toward Zack. "With so much happening at Tomoka Park today, I forgot to mention that ferns were missing from near Oleeta's final resting place. Did you happen to notice?"

Zack shook his head. "I must have been looking at something else."

"Like Oleeta's bikini." Lilli jabbed Zack playfully. "Ranger Al mentioned a special fern that the Timucua turned into bread. I'm going to research Florida ferns and see what turns up."

"He must have been referring to coontie ferns," Kate said. "According to my health magazines, coontie ferns were a source of nutrition for the Timucua."

"Coontie ferns, that's it," Lilli said, and her fingers raced across the computer keys. "Look at this," she said, enlarging a picture on the screen. "The coontie fern, also called the coontie plant, looks like a big turnip."

"According to an article in *Fitfoods* magazine, the Timucua had a very healthy diet," Kate said. "The shoots from sabal palms were their favorite delicacy. I'll try to buy some while you're here. I bet they'd be great in my tofu teriyaki."

"I can't wait for the bikers' barbecue," Zack mumbled under his breath.

"I give up," Lilli said after several tries. "There's nothing about coontie fern poaching."

"I'll look up Ranger Al's number and give him a call," Zack said.

"RANGER AL WAS A BIG HELP," Zack said a few minutes later. "He admitted that just recently he had discovered telltale signs of coontie fern poaching."

"What signs?" Lilli asked.

"Holes in the ground surrounded by shredded leaves. The poachers work so fast chopping away with their machetes and filling their sacks, they don't even bother to cover their tracks. Tomoka Park isn't their only source. They've been randomly hitting many places in Volusia County. According to Al's sources, the going rate for a sack about the size of a pillowcase is thirty dollars."

"Hardly worth killing for," Lilli commented. "What do you suppose they do with the ferns?"

"Al's sources believe that some landscapers, looking for a quick sale of a high-profit item, provide them for clients who want unusual plantings. But there's no proof of any link between local landscapers and fern poachers. As far as Al knows, no one has been accused or arrested."

"Zack, here's something else you should see. I kept thinking about the elephant and monkey designs on the belt buckles, so I checked out animal poaching. Look at this." Lilli began quoting the information. "The trade in plants, wildlife and wild animals is a twenty-billion-dollar-a-year industry. Five millions birds, thirty-two thousand primates."

"I'm following your conversation up there," Lobo called up from the foyer. "My cousin Pablo works with customs at the Mexican border. You wouldn't believe the animal parts people try to sneak past customs. The weirdest was bear gall bladders!"

Lilli gulped. "For what purpose?"

"For medicine," Lobo said. "There are heavy fines and jail time, but people still risk it."

Lilli scrolled through several sites. "I see what Lobo's talking about. Poaching the Grand Canyon's rare Million Butterfly carries a fine of twenty-five thousand dollars and five years in prison."

"And don't forget the parrot cartel," Lobo called up. "Pablo tells me endangered parrots have been smuggled in from Mexico."

"The cruelty and suffering is unbelievable." Lilli sat back, distancing herself from the screen. "I'll spare you these gory details of the greedy poaching business. Suffice it to say that elk are slaughtered for the antlers. Eagles are shot out of the sky for their feathers. Leopards are butchered for their skins. And who can forget the hacked-off hands in *Gorillas in the Mist?* The list goes on. It's sickening."

Zack studied the lists and statistics that Lilli scrolled through. "I have a gut feeling that poaching of plants or animals played a role in the murder in New York City and Tomoka Park. But what could it be? We're missing some vital bit of information to pull it all together."

"I'm going to take a break," Lilli said, rubbing her eyes with the backs of her fists.

"Me, too," Zack said. "Digger promised to get back to us tomorrow. The hotels turned up nothing. Betty knew of only four upcoming events that would bring in visitors. A stamp-collectors' convention and a water-sports convention in Ormond Beach. An antique automobile show and a restaurateurs' convention in Daytona Beach."

"That must be the convention Mrs. D'Amato mentioned," Lilli commented. "Her cousin Luigi is presenting his award-winning mussels marinara."

"Four special events," Zack said, "but nothing related to plants, animals or poaching. Too bad. I thought we might be on the right track."

Kate cleared her throat. "I didn't want to interfere while you were working. Now that you're considering a break, I'd like both of you to listen to what I have to say. It's something I should have admitted years ago. It's about my accident."

"Kate, this isn't the time or place," Zack said. "We'll talk privately. Lilli doesn't need to be part of this."

"You need to hear what I've kept from you all these years," Kate said. "It would be best if you had someone who cares…" She looked at Lilli. "Someone to talk it through with later. I'd like Lilli to stay."

"I don't think that's a good idea," Zack said.

"Please, Zack, let's settle this once and for all," Kate said. "It's affected your work, you told me so yourself. And it's hurting my career as an artist, too. See that stack of mail? It's mostly requests to show my work, but I'm having problems concentrating on business. Please, what do you have to lose?"

"The question is, Kate, what do I stand to gain?"

"How about salvaging your crumbling career?"

Zack's eyes blazed. "You're trying to humiliate me in

front of Lilli, is that what's behind this? You don't want me to be happy because—"

"I didn't want you or anyone else to be happy after my accident. I wanted you and Mom and Dad to suffer."

Zack's stunned look turned angry.

"There, I've said it." Kate's voice wavered. "Isn't this the ugly sort of truth your precinct psychologist wanted you to hear?"

Lilli remembered her promise to herself, to stay clear of any dispute between Zack and Kate. This bedroom had become a minefield on an old family battleground, but if Kate's confession could help Zack, she had to speak up. "Zack, since I've been brought into this, please, as a special favor to me, listen to Kate. Talk to her."

"Two against one." Zack shrugged. "Let's get this over with."

"How about if we go to the back bedroom?" Kate said. "I'd rather Lobo and Mrs. D'Amato didn't hear us."

FOURTEEN

Kate's Confession

ZACK PLUNKED HIMSELF DOWN on the bed and Lilli sat across from him on the rocking chair. Kate remained in the doorway. Did she intend to block their escape or be the first to get away? Lilli wondered.

"I've been unbelievably cruel," Kate began. "I didn't just *allow* people to blame themselves for my accident. I *encouraged* it."

"Please, Kate," Zack said. "Everyone in a wheelchair probably has thoughts like that at one time or another."

Kate held up her hand. "Let me finish. It may seem weird, but letting all of you carry around that burden of guilt gave me control. I called the shots. And I found so many targets." She looked directly at Zack. "You thought your high school graduation brought me home. Mom and Dad thought their wedding anniversary was the culprit. I'm sure the truck driver blamed himself. Even Ted, good old, egotistical Ted, said that if he'd been there entertaining me with his witty banter, I wouldn't have gone jogging."

Kate turned toward Lilli. "Ted was a political colum-

nist I'd been seeing for several years. Mom and Dad
didn't approve. They considered Ted a hard-drinking
man who would break their daughter's heart. We broke
up many times, but I was a slow learner," Kate admitted.
"Then Ted got drunk and abusive at a gallery where two
of my clients were showing their work. That was the
final straw. I couldn't allow him to sabotage my career."
She drew a deep breath and composed herself.

Zack picked up the story. "Two weeks before my
graduation, Kate came home to tell us that she and Ted
were finished. Mom and Dad were thrilled. Kate would
come without him."

"We would all be together, one big happy family,"
Kate said. "But when I walked into the kitchen and
told Mom I intended to give Ted one more chance, we
argued. Every word she said was true, but I defended
Ted. Dad backed up Mom and I argued with both of
them. Finally, I ran out of the house and went jogging
and..." Kate fought back her tears. "I was so angry with
Mom and Dad for telling me what to do. I was mad at
myself, too, for putting up with Ted's rotten temper. I
heard the truck behind me. I heard the horn blasting.
Everyone thinks I immediately got out of the way, but
I didn't." She broke down, sobbing.

"Kate, please stop this," Zack said.

But Kate wouldn't stop. "You can't imagine how
frustrated and angry I was. I didn't move onto the side
of the road. I stopped, turned to that truck and shook
my fist, yelling at the driver to get out of my way and

leave me alone. I didn't care…about anything. Just then a rock bounced up and shattered the driver's windshield. The truck came straight at me. Instinctively I jumped aside, but it was too late. So, now you know what really happened."

Zack knelt in front of Kate and embraced her. "Stop torturing yourself."

Kate pushed him away gently. "You wouldn't believe how many times I've wanted to tell you and Mom and Dad. Every time I look in the mirror, the truth stares back at me. I'm tired of denying what really happened. It wasn't your fault, Zack. Or Mom's or Dad's. Or Ted's. Or the truck driver's. If I had moved onto the shoulder right away…who knows? Or maybe, as my doctors told me, I *was* in the wrong place at the wrong time."

Kate smiled weakly. "Something good came from the accident—losing Ted. Can you imagine me living with a creep like that?" Kate looked at Lilli. "After the accident, Ted insisted on seeing me. No sweet words, no 'I'm sorry about your accident.' He said things had worked out for the best, that I would have slowed him down." Kate's laugh was dry and bitter. "Slow him down. Ted, the journalist, sure had a way with words. My stubborn pride. Thinking I knew Ted better than any of you." She took Zack's hand. "Can you ever forgive me? I was so angry. I took it out on the people I love most. I wanted all of you to suffer. Why should your lives roll merrily along while I could hardly find the energy to sit up in bed?" She laughed and cried at the same time. "Roll merrily along? I'm the one rolling. You're walking."

Zack embraced Kate again and this time she didn't push him away.

Fighting the lump in her throat, Lilli left to allow Zack and Kate a private moment. She went to her bedroom and lay down on the bed, emotionally wiped out by Kate's revelation. Hugging the pillow, she gazed out the window at the darkening sky and thought about her brother Pete.

"It's them against us," Mom used to say to Dad. Pete was Lilli's spokesperson, appealing to their parents to let her extend her curfew, or paint her room purple, or go to Jones Beach for the day with friends instead of studying for finals. And she had done the same for Pete when he came up against their parents' hard-nosed rules.

"What does Pete want now?" Dad would ask when she hung around the breakfast table.

"What does Lilli want?" Dad would ask when Pete stood before him, shuffling from one foot to the other.

Lilli remembered that Dad had commented to Mom at Pete's college graduation, "I'm surprised that neither Lilli nor Pete turned out to be lawyers. They've been practicing since they were kids." Kate's image of the family hanging from a fragile thread crossed through Lilli's mind. The power of parents was strong, but the brother-sister relationship rivaled it.

Lilli heard the elevator door shut. Kate must be going downstairs. There was a gentle knock on her door.

"Come on in," she said softly, opening the door.

Zack stood there without saying anything for a few seconds. Then he swept her into his arms and kissed her passionately. "Sorry to put you through all that," he said. "Dr. Becker, the psychologist, was right. Guilt is a very heavy burden. Kate's going to call our parents and explain everything. This is a new beginning for Kate. And maybe me, too. None of us are ever going to get over that accident, but maybe now we can get beyond it."

Zack kissed Lilli and she couldn't hold back. She had meant her kiss to be gentle, but the passion and longing she felt for Zack exploded. She wanted the moment to go on forever, but she knew better. After several long, thrilling kisses, he pulled away from her. "I know," Lilli said, with a sigh. "It's time for our rendezvous with the bikers."

FIFTEEN

Bulldog

"Be careful," Kate said.

"Don't take any unnecessary risks," Lobo advised. "And remember, Zack, I'm opposed to your taking Lilli along."

Lilli hustled Zack away before he changed his mind. They hurried across the lengthening shadows behind Kate's studio. Mrs. D'Amato's soprano voice cut through the hum of air conditioners and assaulted the high notes of Carmen's tragic life. Lilli imagined Detective John Jones flat on his back on Mrs. D'Amato's couch, nursing a headache and contemplating early retirement.

Leading the way, Zack parted the leaves of the thick hedge of palmettos and entered the bank's parking lot adjoining The Trails. Looking cautiously left then right, Zack unlocked the black Toyota, which Kate's friend, a teller in the bank, had left for them. As an extra precaution, Zack and Lilli had decided not to drive their rental car. They wanted to arrive at Tomoka Park without being followed, park at a safe distance and sneak into biker camp on foot. The biker guy who had demolished their canoe was probably convinced he'd scared them off. But if not? He might follow and drive them off the road, or he might stake out the park entrance and wait for them to arrive. They were alert to either possibility. They figured he wouldn't come after them in biker camp, where they'd be surrounded by Billy Bob, Russell and other rough-and-tumble guys who could hold their own in any fight.

Zack and Lilli pulled out of the parking lot and headed down State Road 40 toward Tomoka Park. Zack constantly checked the rearview mirror. "We'll try all the old tricks," he said, turning up an alley. He back-tracked a few blocks and re-entered the highway.

"No one followed us," Lilli said, glancing at her sideview mirror.

"Good," Zack said. "Let's hope it stays that way."

Lilli and Zack wore dark clothes and running shoes. Nighttime binoculars hung from straps around their necks. "We're going to solve this mystery once and for all," Lilli said, and tugged down a Jaguars baseball cap that trapped her unruly tendrils.

Zack pulled onto North Beach Street. "No one's behind us," he said, checking the rearview mirror again and sounding relieved. They continued for a while in silence, focusing their attention on the dark deserted road. Lilli's neck and shoulders were so tense she couldn't relax them. She wondered if Zack was afraid too, or had he grown accustomed to nerve-wracking investigations?

Zack braked and slowed down. A canopy of trees

loomed overhead, blocking out the stars in the moonless sky. "Let's run through our plan one more time."

"Please, Zack, we've been over it a dozen times."

"I know, but if the right photo opportunity came along you might decide to change our plan. You could become my worst nightmare, a liability."

"No way! I'm an asset. Remember? I spotted the guy with the camera before you did. I uncovered the guy's tattoo and found out it was an orchid. I—"

"Okay, your instincts are good, but you take foolish chances. Promise me if things turn ugly, you'll stay where it's safe. If that's not an option, you'll run for your life."

Lilli put her hands defensively in front of her face. "Maybe I'll throw in some karate chops and kicks, like on TV shows. Have you seen—"

"Listen, Lilli, this isn't TV. There are no retakes if you mess up and no stunt doubles. This is real life and it can get very dangerous."

"Okay, Zack, you win. Here's your plan and I promise to stick to it. We start out doing what's expected. I photograph the biker camp while you jot down names and details for my story. We enjoy the barbecue dinner you've been salivating for. Then when it's time to leave, you con Billy Bob into breaking the bikers' code—"

"Con? You mean I'll use tried-and-true interrogation techniques."

"Right. Your techniques encourage Billy Bob to come up with the name of the maniac in the airboat who tried to frighten us off. I wait with Billy Bob while you search the guy's tent or trailer. You find some kind of proof that will connect him to the murder in Tomoka Park and possibly to the murder in New York City. You photograph the proof, whatever it is, with your secret spy camera."

"Lilli, you are so dramatic. It's a standard thirty-five-millimeter camera with a high-speed lens and high-speed film that works in low light."

"I like the idea of a secret spy camera. It's so daring, so—"

"Enough!" Zack shook his head. "Let's review the rest of our plan."

"Okay. We say good night to our biker friends, return to Kate's and turn over the camera and proof to Lobo. Relying on his precinct's resources and his familiarity with local people and places, he helps you solve this mystery. Did I leave anything out?"

"That about sums it up," Zack said, his voice dripping with sarcasm. He braked the car and slowed down. "Crack open your window and listen for any suspicious sounds." He killed the headlights. The park entrance lay straight ahead, barely visible in the growing darkness.

Lilli leaned close to the window as Zack eased the car forward. Eerie birdcalls echoed through trees that creaked and groaned. Weird croaking and hissing sounds emerged from the greenish-black depths. All sorts of scurrying and flapping and fluttering noises came from shrubs and treetops. Uneasy in such creepy surroundings, Lilli fought the urge to wrest control of the car from Zack. She peered through the black night at the dense foliage along the roadside and the canopy of leaves above.

She felt as if she were trapped in a tunnel, an impenetrable tangle of vegetation that would transport her and Zack into…she didn't know what. A trap set by the biker who drove the airboat? A confrontation with the man with the orchid tattoo? A showdown with the person who dumped the body in the midden mound?

Lilli shuddered. Her old fear of being caught in confining places had just crept back into her life. She wouldn't admit it to Zack. He would probably be content if she would forget about photographing the bikers and wait huddled on the car floor while he went about his police business. That wasn't going to happen. She would steel her nerves, take the photos and help Zack in any way possible.

Zack pulled off the road and turned the car around. He backed in, prepared if necessary for a hasty escape, and parked beneath a clump of cypress trees. Quietly, they closed the doors and locked them. Holding hands, they crept beneath gnarled branches. Advancing a few feet, Lilli and Zack stopped and listened. There were plenty of sounds, all from animals. If anything was tracking them, it wasn't human. They hurried toward the side trail and followed it deeper into the park, toward biker camp.

Soon they heard voices and music and saw faint lights.

"Campfires and guitars. Even a sing-along." Lilli sighed, recalling fond memories of summer camp in upstate New York.

"Not exactly," Zack said waving to Billy Bob, Russell and the other bikers he recognized. "It's more like charcoal grills, violins and classical music."

Stepping past the elaborate sound equipment, Lilli and Zack walked into a circle of light flickering from tiki lanterns strung through the trees. Men and women bikers were busily preparing dinner at their grills. Some sat at picnic tables while others swung in hammocks.

"Come join us," Billy Bob greeted them. "We've been waiting for you. Where's your car?"

"By the front entrance. We're running low on gas and didn't want to push our luck," Zack fibbed.

Russell called out, "This is our typical evening in heaven. We're not shy, Lilli. Shoot away!"

"I'm ready when you are," she said. After chitchatting with the bikers and encouraging them to act natural and ignore the camera, Lilli set to work. She was eager to begin the photo shoot and predicted it would turn out even better than her Wacky Wedding series. But every time a motorhome door slammed or someone revved up a motorcycle, she jumped and had to reshoot. When the biker playing a violin along with the recorded music shrieked off key, Lilli heard the stabbing *Psycho* staccato. She wondered who or what waited for Zack and her in the darkness.

Realizing that her shattered nerves could ruin her

concentration and the shoot, she started again with new resolve. Quickly, she moved from one motor home to the next, photographing family groups, individuals, table settings, grills overflowing with food, hammocks bulging with people, everything and anything, especially bikes. Lots and lots of bikes. *Viewpoint* readers would love the sleek machines with the shiny chrome and customized trim shown off in such an unexpectedly remote setting.

Zack remained at her side, asking questions, jotting down information, making everyone feel at ease. Lilli saw Zack's handsome face illuminated by torchlight. She liked working with him and being with him. Would she ever get to relax with him and enjoy the casual Florida lifestyle?

Russell tugged at Lilli's elbow. "Come see my pride and joy and feel free to photograph every bit of her." He led her and Zack to his motor home and flung open the door.

"Geez!" Zack exclaimed and Lilli gasped. "It's a marvel of technology," she said, eyeing the computer, fax machine, copier, scanner and shredder. Zack was busily checking out the big-screen TV, digital camera, speaker system and every other modern electronic miracle known to the twenty-first century.

"Funny thing is," Russell said, "my stuff hardly compares to Billy Bob's. He set the standard and he keeps raising the bar." He laughed. "I know what you're thinking. Me and Billy Bob and some of our buddies look like hayseeds, down to our last dime. We don't have fancy degrees and corporate jobs, but we got lots of money and enjoy spending it. Biker camp has us rubbing shoulders with some real high-class doctors, lawyers and executives. Their taste for the finer things in life jumped at us like fleas to junkyard dogs." He scratched his arms and laughed. "The biker life isn't just about tearing up the highway. It's about improving yourself."

Lilli enjoyed Russell's wisdom. "I thought you were on vacation," she commented. "What do you do with all this equipment?"

"Are you kidding? I stay in touch with my stock broker, financial analyst and astrologer. I can't afford to miss my biker chat room, one of my best sources for investment tips. Many of the best accountants are bikers."

Lilli photographed Russell's motor home, room by room, marveling at how every nook, cranny and cubbyhole had been utilized for storage. Clutter was minimal. Beds folded up, tables swung down, chairs swiveled, countertop appliances fit snugly into customized spaces. More than once she was fooled by a solid-wood panel that concealed drawers. "Stops everything from flying around when I take a turn real sharp," he explained. Lilli knew that the readers of *Viewpoint* magazine would be delighted with this inside look at the bikers' home away from home.

"I'm done," Lilli said at last and thanked Russell for

his hospitality. She packed up everything except her favorite camera, which she slung over her shoulder.

"What's that for?" Zack asked.

"Just in case."

"In case what?"

"Oh you know, a bear comes charging out of the woods. Or some other unexpected thing happens."

"Lilli, you promised."

"The music surprised me," Lilli said, returning to Billy Bob's site. "I guess I was expecting country or pop."

"I'm no long hair," Billy Bob said sliding his hat forward, "but I'll admit I got hooked on the three B's— Beethoven, Bach and Brahms. Now I'm expanding my horizons, and my alphabet, thanks to my buddies here in camp. Lots of bikers are classical nuts. And I'm not talking about almonds or cashews."

Russell set a large salad bowl on Billy Bob's picnic table. "I told Lilli and Zack we're not all down and dirty types like some folks think. We have our share but hey, if they can afford a Harley they're okay in my book."

"Enough talk, let's chow down," Billy Bob said, ringing a crystal bell. "I've invited several buddies to join us."

Zack sniffed the air. "I don't smell barbecue sauce."

"Barbecue is old hat," Billy Bob said and slapped his thigh. "My little woman would kill me if she heard that. Hats are her way of bringing home the bacon, if you know what I mean." He laughed heartily. "You won't find any barbecue sauce slathered on our food. We're into low-fat cooking and calorie counting."

"I brought along my Caesar salad," Russell said. "I make it with my own croutons from nine-grain bread laced with sun-dried tomatoes, not those dried-out sorry lumps they sell in the store."

"Tonight—" Billy Bob stirred the contents of a crystal bowl nested in an ice bucket "—we have gazpacho soup, followed by lobster kabobs, curried rice and green beans splashed with vinaigrette." He chuckled. "I've given up my old roadkill cooking. Now I can quote pretty darn good from *Road Gourmet* magazine. Me and the little woman are even taking night-school French classes to help with the pronunciation. She's becoming quite the scholar."

"I thought Kate was unique," Zack mumbled to Lilli. "Now I see there's a whole health-nut movement out here and we're caught in the middle of it."

As the meal wound down and the guests headed back to their own campsites, Zack set down his espresso cup. "I'd like to lay my cards on the table," he said to Billy Bob and Russell.

"Five-card stud's my favorite." Russell guffawed.

"Now, Russell, it's plain to see Zack ain't got cards in mind. Trouble's been dogging him since somebody smashed his car window. Go ahead, Zack. You're among friends."

"Okay. There's no way but to come right out and say it. I want revenge. I want it bad and I want it now. I've heard about the bikers' creed, how you stick together and protect your own. But this is different. This is the attempted murder of a helpless little woman, my Lilli."

Lilli flinched at hearing herself used as bait to hook Billy Bob and Russell. That sly old Zack. He accused her of putting business first and doing anything to get a good photo. Ha! He had her beat.

"Let's hear your story," Billy Bob said.

"One of the bikers here in Tomoka Park swamped the canoe Lilli and I were in. Then he tore into it, ripping it apart. We're lucky to be alive. Lilli struggled ashore and more than once I thought she was a goner. Some of the biggest gators I've ever seen came after her. I'd guess there were four or five, but I was too busy rescuing her to count."

"Those big teeth, those whipping tails, those beady eyes. I'll never forget those gators as long as I live," Lilli said. "Thank heavens Zack was there to protect me and drag me out of the water." She tired to sound helpless and scared, playing to their sympathies.

"This guy who tried to kill an innocent woman couldn't be a Harley man," Billy Bob said firmly. "No sir, no way. It's got to be a biker from hell."

"I couldn't get a good look at him," Lilli said, "but he has a mustache and stocky frame. You know, a bull neck and muscular shoulders like a weight lifter. He was wearing a black and white bandana."

"That narrows it to a handful of guys," Russell said. "And they're all from hell."

Lilli snapped her fingers. "I almost forgot. The guy was wearing a spiked dog collar around his neck."

Billy Bob dropped his spoon. "Bulldog Briggs! He's on the fringe of wacko-weird, ready to flip into total freak-out. Nobody trusts him, but they keep him around in case a fight breaks out."

"Stay clear of him and his two buddies," Russell said. "They make Bulldog look like the poster boy for Squeaky Clean soap."

"I'm not going after Bulldog," Zack said. "I've got plans for his bike that will bring him to his knees. Hit where it hurts, that's my motto."

Lilli couldn't believe how quickly Zack came up with creative lies that got him exactly what he wanted. Was he the same way with women? With her?

"What are the buddies' names?" Zack asked.

"I've never had the pleasure of speaking to them," Russell said. "Everybody calls them Greaser and Slime behind their backs."

"Let me guess," Zack said. "Greaser majored in motorcycle maintenance and Slime—"

"You don't want to know," Billy Bob said. "Let's just say he doesn't bathe, wash his clothes or use a handkerchief."

"Not a pretty sight," Lilli commented.

"Or a pleasant smell." Russell pinched his nose.

"Anything else?" Zack asked.

Billy Bob nodded. "They were black and white bandanas and they got shaved heads, just like Bulldog."

Zack leaned closer, his eyes narrowed with determination. "I need to know how far Bulldog and his buddies might go. Do they have criminal records?"

Billy Bob shrugged. "It's a free country. They're allowed in the park same as we are. Heaven, purgatory or hell, we're all bikers and we don't harass each other. As far as I'm concerned, that's the way it should be."

Lilli sensed that Zack had crossed the line. If he pursued his line of questioning, he'd lose Billy Bob and Russell.

"Where's Bulldog's campsite?" Zack asked.

"It's easy to spot. A black and white flag stamped with the face of a bulldog hangs from his motor home's antenna." He pointed beyond the tiki lanterns. "It's due west, along the outer ring of hell, dead center in the back."

"I'll find it," Zack said.

Lilli stood up. "I'm going with you."

"No," Zack said firmly.

"One or two photos, that's all I want."

"You promised to stick to our plan."

"But I didn't know that Bulldog, Greaser and Slime were so...photogenic."

"I hope you're not allowing the little lady to go with you," Billy Bob said.

"Zack, I'd like a word with you in private," Lilli said. She got him alone and said, "You owe me, the helpless and defenseless little woman, for prying information out of these guys."

"You can't come with me and that's final," Zack said. "You heard what rotten guys we're dealing with."

"I can be very persuasive," Lilli said. She threw her arms around Zack's neck and kissed him long and hard. "Care to change your mind?"

"Okay," Zack said, struggling to catch his breath, "but be prepared to hear me talk guy talk and sound like your lord and master." Before Lilli could respond, Zack turned to Billy Bob and Russell. "You know how your gal is about hats, Billy Bob. Well, with my Lilli it's photos. She's got five minutes to snap away. Then, whether she likes it or not, I'm sending her back here. This is a job for a man and she'll be in my way. I'm hoping you'll keep an eye on her."

"Glad to, ole buddy." Billy Bob looked at his watch. "Call for help if you need it. None of us likes going to hell if Bulldog Briggs is within striking distance, but we've got several lawyers here in heaven who've earned black belts. I'm sure they'd jump at the chance to show Bulldog their off-hours version of criminal justice."

"Sounds like they could give karate-kicking and chopping movie stars a run for their money," Lilli said.

"You got that right," Billy Bob said.

Lilli grabbed an extra roll of film from her tote bag. "Okay, Zack," she purred. "Let's go."

SIXTEEN

Hell

LILLI AND ZACK PASSED a cluster of motor homes, tents and bikes, about fifteen minutes from heaven. "Purgatory's quiet. Looks like everybody's in bed," she said. They continued for several more minutes, but didn't see any signs of hell. Lilli began to wonder if they were lost when the pungent smell of decay stung her nostrils.

Soon she and Zack entered a swampy area, filled with wet leaves, rotting vines and slippery moss. The combination would have been treacherous even in broad daylight. Following the swamp's perimeter, they struggled along for several more minutes.

"We're so far from heaven and purgatory," Lilli said.

"I hear men's and women's voices." Zack stopped and looked through his night binoculars. "Hell's up ahead."

Lilli adjusted her binoculars. "I can make out a dozen guys back beyond their campfire, but they all look murky green. I can't tell if anyone's wearing a bandana."

"Let's hope Bulldog and his buddies are there," Zack

said. "We're out of luck if they're inside Bulldog's motor home."

They crept closer. To her left, Lilli saw three bikers throwing knives. Their blades whipped through the air, slicing through a take-out pizza box nailed to a tree. To the right, two bikers wrestled in mud. Several bikers were stretched out in hammocks and snoring like buzz saws. Others had collapsed on top of their sleeping bags. The rest were guzzling beer and tossing the bottles and cans into the shrubbery.

Lilli leaned forward, peering into the green darkness. Three female bikers were passing around a whiskey bottle and tossing back shots. The one with long, stringy hair began dancing to music from a boom box. Lilli figured from the dramatic bump-and-grind routine that the woman was a professional stripper. The other two women clapped their hands and tried to imitate her, but gave up. The one with spiky hair flicked her cigarette lighter and lit up. The flame glinted off the rings pierced through her ears, eyebrows and navel.

Zack signaled Lilli to creep even closer.

"What a nightmarish scene," Lilli whispered, dropping to her knees. Take-out boxes from fast-food places lay scattered on the ground next to plastic knives and forks. Flies buzzed around pizza crusts, chunks of fried chicken, globs of mashed potatoes and half-eaten cream pies. A wood fire in the center of hell sending up whirls of greenish smoke was dying out. No one bothered to replenish it. The main source of light came from flashlights dangling from ropes slung over branches. To Lilli, they looked like voodoo dolls hanging from nooses.

Zack nudged Lilli and pointed to the far left. She peered through her night binoculars and saw a motor home with a black and white flag picturing a bulldog's face hanging from the antenna. There were two doors, both on the driver's side, and they faced the campfire. "Getting inside without being seen will be difficult," Lilli whispered.

"The back door's no good," Zack added. "It's blocked by those two huge garbage cans."

Lilli shuddered, imagining the sound of metal cans knocking in to each other and waking up every biker in hell.

"The front door's the only option, but I don't like it," Zack said. "There's a wire running from the overhead light to the doorframe and on inside. The light could be triggered to go off when the door opens."

"What are we going to do?"

"I'll think of something," Zack said, but he didn't sound too sure of himself.

Hoping to spot Bulldog, Zack and Lilli inched forward.

"You're asking for it!" a gruff voice boomed. Three guys, the size of refrigerators, wearing black and white bandanas charged out of the darkness into the firelight.

"Bulldog." Lilli's whisper crackled with terror.

"Greaser and Slime," Zack said, his voice a mixture of awe and fear. "While all three are in sight, let's work our way over to the motor home."

Stealing further back into the shadows, Lilli watched in horror as Bulldog seized one of the wrestlers by the nape of the neck and smashed his face into a cream pie. "Next time you want seconds, just ask!" Bulldog laughed a hideous laugh. It ended in a series of belches. Lilli's stomach flipped.

As Lilli scurried with Zack in the fringe of darkness toward the motor home, she stole glances at the trio. Greaser picked up the wrestler and hurled him at Slime. Back and forth they tossed him like a football until the wrestler finally collapsed in a heap on the ground. Greaser and Slime slammed each other on the back, like football players congratulating each other on a super play.

"Hey! Knock it off!" Bulldog slung a beer bottle at the line of hanging flashlights, sending wild swirling arcs of light across the camp. "I'm not in the mood to dig a grave for this guy. I'm in the mood for women! Soft naked women, not these tough-skinned biker chicks."

Lilli saw Bulldog's face flash in and out of the streaks of light. His small piggish eyes seemed to disappear between his blubbery cheeks and wide brow. He was worse than the monsters in her scariest nightmares. She wouldn't take one single photograph. Any noise, even the click of a camera, might alert him that someone was nearby. That could mean certain death. Zack pulled her back into the darkest shadows.

When Lilli looked again, Bulldog, Slime and Greaser were guzzling beer and passing around girly magazines. They slapped the pages and laughed big belly laughs.

"They're getting drunker by the minute," Zack whispered. "Let's hope they fall down and sleep on the spot. We'll need all the time we can get." He and Lilli hurried to the far side of the motor home.

The ledges of all three windows were higher than Zack's shoulders. "I'll lift you up," he whispered, cupping his hands. Lilli set her foot in his hands, he boosted her up, and she gripped the window ledge. The interior was partially lit by a lava lamp on the kitchen table. It emitted weird orange and red swirling lights. The furniture, counters and everything else that Lilli could see were black.

"I'm surprised," Lilli whispered. "I expected a sink full of dirty dishes or garbage strewn across the kitchen floor. Let's try the other windows," she whispered.

Zack eased his way along the motor home while Lilli groped her way, hand over hand, to the other two windows. She peered into the living area and bedroom, aglow with flaming colors from lava lamps. "There's some socks, underwear and T-shirts tossed on the unmade bed, but I've seen worse."

"I'm going in," Zack whispered as he lowered Lilli to the ground. "Wait for me over there in the bushes."

"I'm going with you," Lilli whispered. "Bulldog's

place is almost identical to Russell's. I know all the cubbyholes and hiding places. With my help, you'll be in and out with your information in two minutes flat."

"I don't like it," Zack whispered. "Remember our plan—"

"Women have been known to change their mind."

"I don't have time to argue."

"Good."

They waited until Bulldog, Slime and Greaser were facing away from the motor home, then they sneaked along the passenger side and up to the front door. Zack reached up and tried to loosen the light bulb. Stuck in a rusty old fixture, it wouldn't budge. Zack gripped the bulb and turned it hard. It sprang loose, slipped from his hand, and dropped toward the ground. Lilli held her breath, praying the bulb wouldn't hit a rock and startle Bulldog and his buddies. Whew! It landed in a pile of leaves.

Zack had a set of passkeys in his hand, but when he turned the knob the door cracked open. They slipped inside. Zack handed Lilli a pencil-thin flashlight that emitted a compressed beam of light. He had another exactly like it.

Lilli headed for the bedroom. She opened the panels and rifled through the cubicles and drawers. She knew what to look for: photos, negatives, film, address book, a cache of money, lists of gun serial numbers, something connected to Benjamin Voda the cop killer or some link with plant and animal poachers. All she found were playing cards, spare change, poker chips, magazines and rumpled clothes.

Lilli hurried to the living room, where Zack was working his way through Bulldog's computer files. She figured if he found anything relevant, he would copy it onto a disk. She spied a stack beside the printer.

Lilli looked everywhere, but found nothing useful. She carefully put everything back the way it was. Zack had warned her that Bulldog must not suspect that anyone was snooping around. If Bulldog changed plans or ditched information, the investigation would be compromised.

Lilli glanced outside to make sure Bulldog wasn't coming and then methodically worked her way through the kitchen. She opened the cabinet door beneath the sink. Between the roach tablets and mousetraps lay a rolled-up white terrycloth towel. Carefully, she picked it up and lifted back the corners. "Zack, look at this." She held up the towel, revealing a long thin knife with a carved jade handle. Dried blood was caked on the blade.

"Don't touch it," Zack cautioned. He grabbed a clean fork, chipped off several particles of dried blood, and wrapped them in his handkerchief.

"This sure doesn't look like the kind of knife Bulldog would use," Lilli said, noticing the intricate lacy carvings on the jade handle.

"If I'm right, we have our New York connection. I'm

betting this knife belongs to a notorious woman from Chinatown."

"Who?"

"Later. Put the towel and knife back where you found them and see what else you can find. Hurry!"

Lilli checked again to make sure that Bulldog wasn't coming to his motor home. She poked through the rest of the kitchen while Zack finished up with the computer. After checking the last set of drawers, she sighed with disappointment. She'd thought she'd find something. Exasperated, she plunked her hands on her hips. "In the movies, the bad guy always taped the film or whatever to the bottom of a drawer."

"That's just movie stuff," Zack said, thumbing through Bulldog's mail. "It never happens that way during police investigations."

Lilli couldn't resist. She laid on her back in front of the computer station, pulled out each drawer, and aimed her flashlight beam at the bottom. "Nothing," she complained and dropped down in front of the kitchen sink. Her baseball cap slid off and she set it on the counter. Again, she aimed her flashlight at the bottom of the first drawer. Nothing.

She pulled out the second and gasped. "I've got something," she said, looking at sheets of paper taped to the drawer. "Bulldog must have seen the same movies I did."

Zack peeked out the window, then dropped onto his back next to Lilli. "I didn't know I was working with an international spy. Good work," he said and carefully peeled back the tape. "It's a list." He counted. "Twelve pages of names and numbers. Could be license plates. Keep a lookout for Bulldog."

Zack pulled his camera from his pocket and began copying the pages. "Bulldog's coming!" Lilli exclaimed. "Greaser and Slime are with him."

"One minute."

"Hurry, Zack. They're headed this way."

"Four pages to go."

Lilli heard the page turn, the camera click.

"Three pages. Two."

"They stopped. Bulldog is wrestling Greaser. Let's get out of here. Right now."

"One last page."

Lilli turned and saw Zack tape the list back in place.

"Bulldog and his buddies just stopped off at the motor home, two sites away."

"Good. Don't breathe, don't make a sound."

"Don't worry."

Zack cracked open the door. Suddenly, the fax machine whirred. Lilli nearly jumped out of her skin. Zack closed the door soundlessly and hurried to the machine. He photographed the fax as it landed in the tray. "More numbers and names."

Zack cracked the door open again. "Come on," he whispered. Lilli slipped out right behind him and crept toward the bushes.

"Oh no," Lilli said, dropping to her knees and pushing her hair out of her eyes. "I left my baseball cap on Bulldog's kitchen counter. I'm sorry, Zack. I wasn't thinking."

"It's okay," Zack said, but his tone was stern. "I'll go back. Stay here. If I get trapped in there, sneak back to Billy Bob's campsite and have him drive you home."

"What about you?"

"Don't worry. By the time you get to heaven, I'll be right behind you." He handed her his camera. "Give this to Lobo."

Before Lilli could say anything, Zack took off. She peered through the bushes and saw him rush up the steps and sneak inside. Her heart hammered as she heard men's gruff voices. Bulldog, Greaser and Slime were coming back.

Zack was trapped! She must distract them, draw them away, give Zack a chance to escape. But if Bulldog saw her, he would recognize her and figure that Zack was nearby. That could ruin Zack's investigation.

Lilli searched by her feet. Stones. She scooped up a handful of stones. Bulldog was only a few yards from his motor home. She would throw the stones into the bushes to his right to make him think someone was there. She wanted to be brave for Zack's sake, but she froze on the spot, terrorized, imagining what Bulldog might do to her. Her hands trembled and the stones tumbled from her fingers.

"Yo, Bulldog!" Billy Bob walked out of the shrubbery near Lilli, like he was out for an evening stroll. Startled, Lilli nearly cried out.

"Bulldog, you got a minute?" her angel from heaven, Billy Bob, asked. "We need to talk. Your buddies, too." He was trying to draw Bulldog away by talking loud and fast about the guys from hell donating time to the Parade of Toys. Bulldog lumbered toward Billy Bob, who was close to Lilli. He pulled his flashlight from his pocket and checked his watch.

Afraid that Bulldog might see her, Lilli crawled away. Her knee came down hard on a jagged rock. "Aagh!" She tried to stifle her cry of pain, but she was too late.

Bulldog whipped out his flashlight and turned it in her direction. The beam swept through the bushes near Lilli. "Who's there?" he grunted. He'll know he's been spied on, Lilli thought. In only seconds he might drag her out of the bushes. She couldn't escape, but she could make a run for it and if Bulldog chased her, Zack might be able to get away. Her carelessness with her baseball cap had sent Zack into danger. Maybe now her boldness could get him out.

She was summoning her courage when Russell stepped from behind her. "Hey, Bulldog, don't worry. It's only me, Billy Bob's buddy," he said.

Billy Bob and Russell were her bodyguards, her saviors! They talked to Bulldog about the toys. Bulldog checked his watch several times as if he were going to be late for a date. Lilli turned her night binoculars toward the motor home door. It inched open. Billy Bob and Russell were talking real loud to mask any noise that Zack might make. Zack stepped out, closed the door behind him, crouched down and slithered into the bushes. Seconds later, he made it to Lilli's side and set her Jaguars cap on her head.

"I smell a rat!" Bulldog sniffed the air. He wiped his nose on the back of his hand.

"Hey, Parade of Toys is a legitimate cause." Billy Bob shook his head.

"No. I smell a real rat," Bulldog said. "A rat who thinks he's gonna finish off the pizza and chicken. Well, he'll have to fight me for it." Bulldog pulled a knife from his belt and stomped toward the campfire. "I'll let you know about the toys," he called over his shoulder.

Lilli and Zack's breathing returned to normal. Billy Bob and Russell hurried toward them. Russell said, "Let's get out of here."

"I owe you one," Zack said.

"Me, too," Lilli added. She turned to Zack. "Now when we send our friends postcards, we can say 'We've been to hell and back.'"

SEVENTEEN

Poachers in The Park

"THE SOONER WE GET OUT of here, the better," Zack said as he and Lilli retraced their steps from heaven to their car. "With Lobo's help, we'll find the missing pieces that link Bulldog, Tomoka Park and New York City."

Lilli swatted away a branch and hiked her tote bag over her shoulder. "I hope Bulldog doesn't notice that somebody has been snooping around. Do you think he'll come looking for us?"

"No, not that jerk. He's probably passed out by now."

"Uggh! After wrestling the rats for his dinner." Lilli trotted along, trying to keep up with Zack.

"Let's take the main trail," Zack said, veering to the right. "I think it's faster than the way we came. There's not so much underbrush."

Lilli looked over her shoulder. "And less chance of an ambush if Bulldog gets wise to us."

They stopped to catch their breath where the trail split into two, one going to the boat launch area, the other toward the main entrance.

"That's odd," Lilli said. "The moonlight is glinting

off something over there just off the trail." She peered through her night binoculars. "It's a van, but I don't see the driver."

"There's must be a dozen bicycles leaning against it," Zack said, adjusting his night binoculars. "I'm going to check it out."

"You mean 'we're going'," Lilli said.

Zack sighed. "Arguing with you is a lose-lose situation."

They crept toward the van.

Lilli stopped when she heard branches crackling. "Something's moving through the underbrush. Coming this way."

Lilli and Zack ducked back into the bushes.

"Over there," Zack whispered. "A line of people."

"Twenty," Lilli counted with the help of her binoculars. "They've got sacks slung over their shoulders."

"All except the first guy, the leader of the pack." Zack said. Lilli focused on the lanky man in jeans, plaid shirt, cowboy boots and hat. He towered over the others. "He's got a clipboard in his hand."

"A pencil-pushing cowboy," Zack said.

They followed at a safe distance behind the men, who scurried through the trees. A low chirp sliced through the air, mixing with other night sounds.

"A signal," Zack said. "Let's see what it means." He and Lilli waited and watched.

The men fanned out, forming a large circle. When they were several yards apart, they dropped their sacks, and shone their dim flashlights at the ground. They bent down and yanked up plants. They hacked away the leaves with their machetes and stuffed the booty in their sacks.

"Coontie ferns," Lilli said. "I'm sure of it."

Quickly and quietly, the men repeated the digging and stripping until they had filled their sacks. Then each picked up his two remaining empty sacks and moved toward the center of the circle. The flashlight beams moved closer together, closing in the circle, casting eerie pale green streaks into the gloomy green of the night binoculars. The drifting greens, merging and then separating in ever-changing patterns, created a spooky sub-aquatic scene, as if a giant aquarium had dropped down into the park.

In the distance, the river lapped the docks and boats. Boaters…river…alligators. Panic gripped Lilli. Did alligators crawl onto riverbanks and slither into underbrush to hunt human prey? Her knee had bled when she hit the jagged rock back at Bulldog's. Did alligators sense the presence of blood and track down their victims, like sharks and piranha? Perspiration and the humid night air coated Lilli's face with a slick mask. She wiped her forehead with the back of her sleeve and shifted from foot to foot.

"Simmer down," Zack said. "You'll be back at Kate's, enjoying a nice soothing shower, before you know it. Or, we could go for a late-night swim."

"Are you crazy?" she snapped. "We could run into alligators."

"In Kate's pool?"

"They're everywhere. They could be crawling toward us right now."

"Journalists," Zack muttered. "Their imaginations run wild at the worst possible times."

Finally, the men had filled their sacks and hoisted them onto their backs. Bent over with the weight of their stolen cargo, they headed back the way they had come. The cowboy led the way.

"We can get to the van before they do," Zack said. "I want to get a better look at the cowboy. He must be driving the van."

"I'm curious about the bicycles," Lilli said. "First it was bikers with motorcycles. Now it's poachers with bikes."

"I thought you were going to tell me that gators were pedaling the bikes around the park."

"Are you making fun of me?"

"Heck no. It sounds like a good idea for a new Disney adventure ride."

They crept up to the rust-dappled mud-splattered van, and looked inside. There was only the driver's seat and foam mattresses covering the floor.

Zack checked both front and rear license plates. "How convenient. They're covered with mud." He rubbed his hands on the moist grass and wiped the rear plate. The letters spelled out MY GIRLS. "That's a familiar combination. I'm quite sure it matches the first line on Bulldog's list."

Lilli snapped photos of the van, the license plate, and the bicycles. Twigs cracked and leaves rustled. "They're getting close," Zack whispered. "Don't chance any more flash pictures." They hid behind a clump of yucca plants, and watched.

The poachers were wiry and short. Lilli picked up a word or two of Spanish and several words that sounded like Chinese. She couldn't see their features. They lined up behind the van, speaking softly to each other. One by one, they loaded their sacks in the van. The cowboy checked them off the sheet of paper on his clipboard. He handed each man several dollar bills.

Suddenly, a stocky figure jogged up to the truck.

"Bulldog," Lilli whispered. She and Zack flattened themselves on the ground and peered through the sword-shaped leaves of the yucca.

The cowboy handed Bulldog a large wad of bills. Bulldog counted them out and shoved them in his pocket. Quickly counting the men and sacks, he punched information into his Palm Pilot. Then he took off and disappeared into the bushes.

"So the pecking order is lowly poacher, middleman truck driver and top-of-the-heap Bulldog. Bulldog, the collector, with a Palm Pilot. I didn't think he could read or write, let along count above three."

"Something's fishy," Lilli said. "Bulldog's not drunk. And back at his motor home, he kept looking at his watch. He didn't want to be late for this meeting. That story about the rats was all an act to get rid of Billy Bob and Russell. I wonder if he's deceiving Greaser and Slime or if they're in on this, too."

"He's up to his eyeballs in this Tomoka business," Zack said, "but he's got a good cover going for himself."

"Do you think he killed the man in the midden mound?"

"Probably," Zack said. "And I'd bet my life savings he's involved somehow with Madame Kwan, the owner of the jade-handled knife. She's Chinese and I'd guess so are some of those poachers."

The cowboy spoke to the poachers and then got into the van. With his headlights off, he headed slowly back down the road. "We'll try to catch up with the cowboy later," Zack said. "If we lose him, we can find him through his license plate. Let's see what's up with the poachers."

The twenty men lined up their bikes single file. A timid voice counted off the seconds in Spanish, followed by Chinese. Every third seconds, a poacher jumped on his bicycle and pedaled soundlessly into the darkness to make his way out of the park.

"I guess they're making sure no one crashes into anything," Zack said. "Every move seems practiced. They've done this before and they could do it again. The park's so large the rangers won't notice the theft for days."

"The bikes are a clever strategy," Lilli said as the last poacher passed by. "No lights, no engine noise, no unusual late-night traffic to alert the people who live along the road."

"They must have a rendezvous place. Let's get to our car and follow them."

AFTER TEN MINUTES of driving, Zack pulled over and slammed his fists on the steering wheel. "We lost them! Where could they have gone?"

"Must be they didn't head back toward Ormond Beach," Lilli said. "What if they turned right outside the park?"

Zack thought for a moment. "That's it. They're on their way to Bulow Plantation, a few miles up the road. They'll meet up with that same van or another van and poach more plants." He pulled back onto the road. "Let's leave the poachers for now. We need to work on Bulldog's list!"

EIGHTEEN

Madame Kwan

FIGHTING THE SUNLIGHT that gleamed through the vertical blinds, Lilli turned over and groaned. Every muscle in her body screamed for attention. She cracked open one eye and looked at the clock on the night table. It was 8:30! The aroma of freshly brewed coffee pulled her from the tangle of sheets where she had wrestled slithery alligators and vicious bulldogs through the night. Whew! She was grateful to have escaped a sinister fog-bound world where creeping vegetation snared her legs, salivating animals attacked and apparently no men dared to roam. Her dreams were starting to resemble her past year: few men, not much romance.

Why couldn't she fall asleep and turn into one of those romantic heroines who had the good sense to race across the swirling mists of the moors into the arms of an adoring man? Standing in the shower, she envisioned herself headed for such a rendezvous wearing a romantic blouse with dozens of tiny buttons marching down the front, a skirt supported by voluminous crinolines, dainty shoes, a flowing cape and a bonnet tied over her intricately braided upsweep. "Heathcliff," she murmured into the soap bubbles popping up from her body scrub and imagined the sound of his name carrying over the wind and rain.

Lilli stepped out of the shower and into reality. In two minutes flat, she fluffed her hair, threw on a T-shirt and pair of shorts, and laced up her hiking boots, which were still damp and definitely odoriferous.

She hurried downstairs where Zack, Lobo and John stood hunched over the dining room table. They looked up from the mess of manila envelopes, folders, computer printouts and coffee mugs, and nodded a sleepy-eyed good morning. Zack's welcoming smile made Lilli wish that every morning began with him by her side. He wasn't Heathcliff. He wasn't movie idol Harrison Ford. But, oh my, he was a keeper.

"Sorry to be such a sleepyhead," Lilli said. "Swimming and running in my hiking boots wore me out."

"Try some of Kate's Jamaican Blue coffee," Zack advised, filling a mug from the steaming carafe. "You'll feel like your old perky, feisty self in no time." He handed her the mug and gazed into her eyes. "A nerve-jangling mug of coffee and a perky, feisty woman. My favorite way to start the day."

"In that order?" Lilli asked.

"Knock it off, you two," Lobo said, "or we'll never finish these lists." Lilli heard the curtness in his voice and wasn't sure if he was teasing.

"What have you got there?" Lilli asked, blowing the steam off her coffee.

Lobo thumped several sheets with his pen. "Bank accounts. License plates. Passenger lists, hotel reservations. We've got a pretty good picture of what's going on at Tomoka Park."

John added, "We're still missing some pieces, but we're much closer than we were yesterday at this time."

"We're waiting for some last-minute info from Digger, my friend at the New York precinct," Zack said. "Then we're ready to roll."

Lilli looked from one sheet of paper to the next. "You must have worked through the night."

"We had to," John said. "We're in the middle of a crime web that stretches from Asia to America, from New York to Florida, with who knows how many stops in between."

"And the mastermind of it all?" Zack riffled through the manila envelopes. "The infamous Madame Ming-Húa Kwan, an exotic beauty from China."

"Is she the woman who owns the knife we found in Bulldog's motor home?" Lilli asked.

Zack nodded. "And the blood on the blade matched up with Ronny Miller, the dead man dumped in the midden mound."

"Madame Kwan is evil to the core." Lobo scowled. "She put the 'fatal' in 'femme fatale'."

Zack gathered several envelopes. "You were right, Lilli, when you figured the Tomoka and New York murders involve plant and animal poaching. But it goes beyond that to protection rackets and money lending and ends up in human smuggling and slavery, all organized by Madame Kwan. She has capitalized on illegal immigrants' search for the American dream and turned it into their worst nightmare. Every police officer in New York City has heard of her and now she's been sighted in Florida."

"Where?" Lilli asked.

"According to the FBI, who arrived in Daytona Beach last night, Madame Kwan moved her brother and six cousins into a mansion in Orlando several weeks ago." He tapped the envelope marked Airlines. "We know she booked a flight to Daytona Beach and will be arriving there late this morning and staying at the Paradisio Suites, the swankiest hotel in the area."

Zack fanned the envelopes across the table. "If you read all these, you'd find that Madame Kwan entered the U.S. illegally in the 1980s and opened a small import shop in New York City on the fringe of Chinatown. With the help of neighborhood gangs, she began a protection racket, and worked her way block by block throughout most of Chinatown. She obtained naturalization papers, illegally, of course. Soon after, she smuggled groups of Chinese people to Mexico and Central America, bribed officials, provided fake papers, got the immigrants into the United States, and brought them to New York City. Before long, she expanded her business and smuggled Central and South Americans into the States, shipping them in cargo containers on old freighters."

"And no one tried to stop her?" Lilli asked.

"Those that tried were eliminated. Many defended her because she had reunited countless families. She could be very generous, if it suited her purposes. And very lethal, if crossed."

"We think Madame Kwan is behind poaching the parks in the northwest," Lobo added. "Rumor has it she's been bringing illegal immigrants through Canada into the United States and forcing local people to hire them."

John poked his head into the room. "Now she's got her hooks into Florida."

"She's ruthless," Zack said. "She opened a restaurant in New York City as a front for her 'bank.' She lends money to people who want to come to the United States. Her high interest fee keeps those people working for her for years in sweatshops and restaurants. The employers give her a cut. She's made millions."

"I assume she never got caught," Lilli commented.

"She's been convicted of bribery and smuggling, but because of technicalities she only served a few months' jail time." Zack opened an envelope and slid out a glossy black and white photograph. "Here's Madame Kwan with her typical come-hither look and sexy clothes. Youthful looking, beautiful and deadly as a scorpion."

"Let me see." Lilli plucked the photo from Zack's fingers and looked closely. How old was Madame Kwan? she wondered. Hard to tell from the photo. Glamorous. Mysterious. Downright sexy, regardless of her age.

Aha! The photo had obviously been touched up. Madame Kwan was probably older and less beautiful than she appeared. She was no doubt one of those camera-shy people who hated candid shots. Knowing the camera didn't lie, Madame Kwan relied on a touched-up photo's artful deception. Well, Lilli thought, let me photograph her and the truth will come right through.

Lilli studied the immaculately dressed and groomed Madame Kwan. She wore a form-fitting long silk dress with an embroidered bamboo design. Two lacquered hair ornaments, the size of chopsticks, crisscrossed through the snaky coil of thick lustrous hair piled high on her head. Penetrating eyes, set beneath highly arched brows, dominated her nose and delicate mouth. Cold reptilian eyes, Lilli thought. Cold and calculating, observing her prey, waiting for just the right moment. And then those eyes would narrow and she could strike. Get a grip, Lilli told herself. Madame Kwan had intentionally posed in a sinister manner, hoping for the very effect she had achieved.

Lilli chuckled. "Madame Kwan looks like one of those villains from a James Bond movie. Is she for real? Velvet platform shoes. Alligator purse. And check out those kimono-style sleeves." Lilli rolled her eyes. "Very theatrical."

"Make no mistake, Lilli." Zack replaced the photo in the envelope. "She's a gangster and she'll murder anyone who gets in her way. Those sleeves you noticed come in handy for concealing her calling card, matching knives with jade handles." Zack's index finger tapped the center of his chest. "Her knives have frequently been found pierced through the heart of an enemy."

Lilli's eyes went big and wide. "The body in the midden mound! That was Madame Kwan's handiwork."

"We think so. But proving it is another matter. She always has an alibi. She's never come up on murder charges or even conspiracy to commit murder. We figure Bulldog pulled the knife from the body of Ronny Miller in the midden mound and kept it for a souvenir. The lab did a rush job for us. The blood sample matched up."

"Ronny Miller's body was covered with knife wounds," Lilli said. "You thought it was the work of several people."

Zack nodded. "We assume Bulldog received help from some of Madame Kwan's squadron of bodyguards. Take a look at a typical twosome." Zack slid another photo toward Lilli. "They are nasty little vixens with special talents for coercing information."

Lilli peered at the photo. The two women, wearing silk dressed with slits reaching above their knees, showed off their shapely legs. Lilli winced. Perfect bodies with zero body fat. And their smug expressions indicated they knew it. "With those Cheshire grins, they look like contented kittens."

"Kittens? You got that right," Zack said. "They clawed their way to the top. And like their mentor, Madame Kwan, every one of them is proficient with knives."

Lobo added, "Madame Kwan has been quoted as saying that knives are better than guns."

John nodded. "She boasts that knives are silent and never jam."

"If she's ever caught without her knives or body-guards, it's open season and she's fair game for all her enemies." Zack handed Lilli another photo. "Here's Madame Ming-Húa Kwan and her little black book in her New York City restaurant, named after herself—Ming-Húa, Tomorrow's Flower."

Lilli looked at the fuzzy amateurish black and white photo. Madame Kwan sat alone at a corner table. The candlelight flickered, reflecting in her ferocious eyes. Her expression of utter contempt held the promise that something evil was about to transpire. Lilli noticed that the book, no larger than a deck of cards, was held shut with velvet ribbons.

"If we could get our hands on that book, we'd be able to nail her on something big, like murder. I'm sure of it," Zack said.

"Madame Kwan certainly is a strange mix," Lilli mused. "She seems sophisticated, yet her book, wrapped tight with ribbons, reminds me of a schoolgirl's diary."

"I'll wager its contents aren't a schoolgirl's dreams," Zack said. He checked his watch. "You and I will be leaving soon for Frank Culhane's place."

"Who's Frank Culhane?"

"The owner of the van we saw in Tomoka Park last night."

"So that was his license plate number on the top of Bulldog's list, just like you thought," Lilli commented. Zack shot her a look that told Lilli not to say anything else about Frank Culhane. She wondered why. Lobo cleared his throat and began stacking the folders.

"You need a good healthy breakfast after what you've been through," Kate said, wheeling her way in from the kitchen. "Sorry to say, I can't help you out in the health department. John insisted on being the chef this morning and he's a big fan of high-cholesterol cuisine. Everyone except me seems thrilled with his buttery biscuits, fried bacon, fried sausage, fried eggs—"

"Come on, Kate." John smiled, apparently glad to leave Zack and Lobo to their papers and photos. "Don't forget the vegetables."

"Right. Fried potatoes with fried onions and peppers."

John cocked his eyebrow. "And what was your comment when you tasted them?"

"Okay, John, I said they were good." Kate smiled at John and then turned to Lilli. "Would you believe that John was an artist before he became a policeman?"

"Not oils and pastels, like Kate," John said apologetically.

Lilli was dying to know more about Culhane, but she feigned interest in John and Kate's conversation.

"Tell Lilli about your work," Kate encouraged.

John shrugged. "There's not much to tell. I started with graphics and moved into metal sculptures."

"Details," Kate said. "Women love to hear details."

Lilli would have preferred details about Culhane.

"Okay," John said. "I was living in Miami then, but never part of the art scene. I was too busy collecting scrap metal from garbage dumps and hauling it to my garage. Amazing what you can construct from mangled car bumpers and broken picnic sets. One critic called my work 'Junkarama'."

"I read that review," Kate said protectively. "The critic also said your work showed heart."

"How did you end up as a detective?" Lilli asked, wanting to steer the conversation back to the investigation. She stole a glance at Zack and Lobo. The tension between them rippled across the table. She caught a few of Lobo's words—FBI, Culhane, withholding information—all muttered between clenched teeth.

Lilli turned her attention back to John, who seemed to be leading her away from the investigation. "As a favor to a buddy, I helped the police with a sketch of a killer," John said. "More work came my way and I realized how much I enjoyed being involved when big messy cases were just starting. It was like gathering the scraps for my sculptures, but better. It involved people. So I ended up at the police academy and here I am."

Kate handed Lilli a plate and motioned her toward the counter, where food sat on a warming tray. She whispered to Lilli, "Lobo butted heads with the FBI agents who came in on the case in the middle of the night. He's taking it out on Zack. John's staying clear of the whole thing. Zack will explain." In a louder, cheerful voice she said, "I've promised John that when this Tomoka mystery is over, I'm going to introduce him to my friends down at the Salty Creek workshops. They create works of art with metal and would enjoy getting him involved during his free time. He shouldn't let his talent go to waste."

John fiddled with his collar. "When I came here and saw Kate's paintings, I couldn't believe it. Me, talking to Katherine Lee, the famous artist, discussing technique and composition and light. Junkarama John meets beautiful painter, Katherine Lee. I'll never forget this."

Kate patted John's arm. "John doesn't know it, but he's given me some ideas for a series. Something edgier, grittier. We'll see where it goes."

The phone rang and Lilli heard Zack talking to his friend Digger. "I'd better eat," she said, piling her plate with eggs and sausages. "It looks like Zack's about to leave and he's not leaving without me." She speared a forkful of eggs. "Delicious," she commented and dove into the sausage. She would have complimented John, but he was talking to Kate and enjoying every minute of it. Their mutual admiration and growing friendship was apparent. Obviously they had been getting to know each other while she and Zack had been roaming around Tomoka Park.

Lilli sighed contentedly, knowing that Kate was becoming interested in a man besides her brother Zack. Jealousy, good old jealousy. It had a way of popping up unexpectedly, like burned offerings from the toaster. And it only happened when you were late for work, famished, and those were the last two slices of bread in the house.

"Too bad," Zack was saying to Lobo and John. "Digger's inside info doesn't add much. He found out that Madame Kwan keeps her black book with her at all times because she doesn't trust hotel safes."

"Any idea where she keeps it?" John asked. "My guess, it's tucked inside those sleeves along with her knives."

"No," Zack said. "It's in the black alligator purse we saw in the photo. Oh, the other thing that Digger found out? She's allergic to certain perfumes, heady ones, especially with the scent of roses. Digger apologize for making us wait for useless crap like that."

Lilli washed down the last bite of eggs and sausage with a swig of coffee.

"Lilli," Zack called out. "We need to get going to Frank Culhane's. Bring your cameras."

"Any chance I'll be photographing Madame Kwan today?"

"You won't be getting close to Madame Kwan," Zack called out. "With any luck, I will. And I am truly looking forward to the experience."

"You can have the fun of frisking her," John said. "I'll watch…from a distance, far from her knives." He smiled. "But close enough to see that perfect face."

Uggh! That Kwan woman, Lilli thought, taking the

stairs two at a time to her bedroom. She casts a spell over men. They fear her, but she fascinates them. What was her secret? Power, she decided. Wasn't power considered an aphrodisiac? If only it could be bottled and sold over the counter, she'd be first in line.

Lilli shouldered her tote bag bulging with cameras and film. Passing the bathroom, she stopped in her tracks and looked at the vanity where several bottles of cologne poked out of her cosmetic case. She strode to the vanity and chose the Bouquet of Roses cologne. She sprayed it on her wrists. Hmmmm. Delightfully heady. Everything was coming up roses. What the heck! She tossed the cologne into her tote bag. "I'm ready," she called down to Zack, patting the bottle. Ready for anything.

NINETEEN

Frank Culhane

LILLI FASTENED HER SEAT BELT as Zack backed out of Kate's driveway. "What's going on?" she asked. "Kate said Lobo's having a problem with the FBI. What's that all about?"

"They think Lobo's too close to the whole mess to be objective."

"I must be missing something here," Lilli said.

Zack pulled out of The Trails and turned onto State Road 40. "Frank Culhane's a widower doing his best to raise two young daughters—that explains his MY GIRLS license plate. He's planning to marry Lobo's sister, Consuela. Lobo approves. He and Frank are buddies. They play in that basketball group I told you about that meets at the Recreation Center. I've met Frank there once or twice, but I don't know him very well. The FBI claim that several weeks ago Lobo overstepped his authority and helped Frank out of a sticky situation."

"You mean Frank is a suspect. What do they have on him?"

"It's a bit complicated. I'd better explain how things are. Frank was caught between a rock and a hard place after his wife died. Money was tight. He couldn't afford childcare or nursery school while he ran his small trucking business, supplying local restaurants and flea markets with fruits and vegetables. He borrowed money from Lobo and put the girls in nursery school. That's where he met Consuela, one of the teachers. Of course, he probably would have met her through Lobo eventually."

Zack pulled onto Route 95, the fastest way to the cutoff between Tomoka Park and Bulow Plantation. "One day at the flea market, Frank saw a stack of bills, fifteen hundred dollars to be exact, at a vendor's open cash register. Frank lost his senses and took the money. By the time he got to his truck, he realized he'd made a mistake. He went back to return the money. Meanwhile, the guy had called the police and reported the theft. Frank called Lobo. Lobo pulled a few strings and convinced the vendor not to press charges. Frank promised to keep out of trouble. The FBI doesn't miss a trick. The agents found out that Lobo had covered up a criminal matter for his future brother-in-law."

"So the FBI thinks that Lobo's judgment might be clouded and they don't want him negotiating anything with Frank."

"You got it," Zack said, downshifting and passing a slow-moving truck.

Lilli gripped the handrest. "But Lobo straightened out that mess and Frank promised to mend his ways…so why did Frank get involved with the illegal immigrants who were poaching ferns from Tomoka Park?"

"According to the FBI, Madame Kwan had sent one of her thugs, Edwin Jackoby, nicknamed Jackal, to the Ormond Beach area to start a protection racket at flea markets. Jackal heard about Frank and saw an opportunity. He paid Frank a visit and threatened to harm his daughters if he didn't pay protection money himself and encourage his vendors to pay up, too. Frank refused and threatened to go to the police. Jackal tossed Frank's girls in his truck and took them for a joyride. Frank was frantic until the girls were found unhurt. The police promised to protect the girls, but the next day, there was a bomb threat at the girls' school. In the confusion, Jackal grabbed the girls, drove them to the town dump, and left them there. Frank couldn't take another chance. He caved in."

"He must have been scared out of his mind."

"He still is." Zack changed to the left lane and picked up speed. "But he's agreed to talk to me."

"Don't take offense," Lilli said. "But I'm surprised the FBI didn't pull rank and handle this themselves."

"You mean how come they're calling in a New York City detective?"

"Yes," Lilli said meekly, hoping she hadn't hurt Zack's feelings.

"The FBI tried. Agent Douglas Drambetsky is with Frank now, but he's not getting anywhere. I'm the last resort, not their first choice. Frank remembers me from our basketball games and he says he'd rather talk to me than the FBI agents. They don't like my butting in—especially Agent Drambetsky—but to speed things along, they said okay." He glanced at Lilli. "They have their reasons for letting you come along, too."

"I can't wait to hear this," Lilli said eagerly.

"To them, you're an asset. They heard how you helped the Grayrocks Police Department catch the killer who was terrorizing Long Island."

"But, Zack, you were the one who actually caught him."

"With your help. They think you motivate me to dig up answers. The FBI considers us a team."

"A team. You and me. Faraday and Masters. We sure sound good together," Lilli said cheerily. "Don't you agree?"

Zack's jaw tightened. "Forget about us...for now. We have to concentrate on Frank Culhane."

"But, Zack, think how romantic the FBI agents are. They're matchmakers, bringing us together and..." Lilli caught Zack scowling. Men, for gosh sakes! They can only concentrate on one thing at a time. "Right," Lilli said firmly. "Let's think how scared Frank Culhane must be about his girls and their future. He's in way over his head."

"Lobo says he's a great guy. But he's no match for Madame Kwan. She'll do whatever it takes to convince locals to employ her illegal immigrants. It's too lucrative a business for her to abandon. She's got thugs like those bikers, Slime and Greaser, and that goon, Jackal, on her payroll. When Jackal confronted Frank, Frank agreed to Madame Kwan's wish list. So Frank transported the poachers to parks throughout Volusia County, checked in with Bulldog, and delivered the goods to a drop-off point. He hired illegal immigrants to pick fruits and vegetables for his customers. He even housed the immigrants in his barn."

"What he did was wrong, but it's hard to blame him," Lilli said, glad to see their exit was coming up soon. "The lives of his girls were at stake."

Zack nodded. "Frank was warned that if he wanted to see smiles on his girls' faces, he'd better convince the flea market vendors to pay protection. Madame Kwan tries every angle. She's a real piece of work."

"I take it Frank has information the FBI needs."

Zack swerved into the right lane. "The FBI wants an airtight case against Madame Kwan. They've got plenty on her, but they want solid evidence so that this time she can't slip through loopholes. Every criminal activity we can nail her on, big or small, will help put her away for that much longer. They think Frank hasn't shared everything, that he's holding back."

Zack exited from Route 95 and immediately they were in a shady, rustic area similar to Tomoka Park. "In my opinion, Frank's worried about his kids, he's overwhelmed by the FBI and he can't think straight." Zack turned onto Old Dixie Highway. Signs pointed north to Bulow Plantation and south to Tomoka Park.

"Frank's walking a tightrope without a safety net. If I can win Frank over, he might reveal something that's been locked away."

Zack slowed down. "This is Frank's place," he said and turned at a break in the rusted fence onto a dirt road. "It's what travel books call 'Old Florida.'"

A rambling clapboard house with a shady front porch stood in the middle of a ranch-like compound. A rope swing hung from a branch of a cypress tree in the front yard, a mere scattering of weeds and scrabble grass. To the rear, Lilli glimpsed a stable, dilapidated barn, tool shed and chicken coops, nestled beneath dozens of cypress trees. "This place must have been beautiful once," she mused.

Zack parked in back, near the tool shed. A scooter and tricycle leaned against the back-porch steps.

"Are the girls here?" Lilli asked.

"No. They're with Consuela at her apartment, under police protection." Zack glanced over his shoulder at the barn. An expression of disgust clouded his face.

Lilli followed his gaze and saw a dozen or so illegal immigrants in handcuffs, with fear written all over their faces. They clung to each other in small groups of twos and threes, just inside the open doors. FBI agents supervised the tagging of their meager possessions and bicycles. For once, Lilli didn't have the urge to grab her camera and start snapping photographs. "What a sad sight," she said, observing the gaunt people with sunken cheeks, shuttered eyes and stooped shoulders.

"The immigrants are speaking through interpreters to FBI agents," Zack said, heading toward the back porch. "I doubt they'll say anything to incriminate Madame Kwan. She brought them to America and they'll show their gratitude by not implicating her." He walked up the porch steps. "Rounding up immigrants is a rotten job and the FBI agents hate it. They know that to Madame Kwan the immigrants are only ciphers in her account books, not flesh and blood people. She's making millions off their labor."

Lilli realized how difficult it must be for detectives to maintain any sense of idealism, faced with the sad reality of worker exploitation. "There's no choice," she said. "They'll be deported, won't they?"

"As soon as possible." Zack rapped his knuckles on the door. "When you see the immigrants like this, helpless and frightened, about to be herded into vans and taken away, it's important to keep in mind that Madame Kwan is responsible for their suffering. Not the FBI, not the immigration officers. We'll get her. It's just a matter of time. And Frank may be our best hope."

A tall man with angular features and wavy gray hair opened the screen door and stepped onto the back porch. "I'm Agent Douglas Drambetsky," he said curtly, acknowledging Lilli and Zack with a nod. "Frank Culhane will come out soon, but first I want to set the record straight. Listen good, Faraday." His eyes narrowed. "When you work in my territory, you report all your findings to me. Not to Detective Lobo Cruz, not to the

Ormond Beach Police chief, not to your boss back in New York City. Only to me. Do I make myself clear?"

"Perfectly clear," Zack said through clenched teeth.

"The same goes for you, Miss Masters. I heard how you helped this hotshot detective crack a big case on Long Island a few months ago. But that doesn't mean you'll be a superstar here—"

Zack fumed. "Back off, Drambetsky—"

"No, you back off, Faraday." Agent Drambetsky poked his finger in Zack's face. "So you shot some hoops with Frank Culhane. Big deal! This is a criminal investigation, not a basketball game. Your being here isn't worth diddlysquat in my book. The FBI doesn't need a New York City detective…or a nosy photographer—to crack this case."

"You better watch your mouth," Zack snarled.

Agent Drambetsky threw up his hands. "So prove me wrong and give me something to work with."

"I'll do my best," Zack snapped. "And so will Lilli."

To Lilli, a gauntlet had been thrown. A toss of her fiery-red curls signaled that she accepted the challenge. She would listen to everything Frank Culhane told Zack and count on her woman's intuition to kick in. Several female FBI agents were questioning the immigrants, but they weren't close enough to hear Frank and Zack. This was a unique opportunity and she wouldn't let it pass by. She would catch something—a significant detail, or connection or coincidence—that would help the FBI agents with the case. Nosy photographer? Ha! She'd show that insolent Agent Drambetsky...

Agent Drambetsky passed by, muttering under his breath about a pesty redhead wasting his time, and strode to the far end of the porch. Lilli curled her fists to hold her temper in check. While she fumed, he jiggled the rainspouts as if he were a building inspector, not an agent guarding a prime witness in a federal case.

Lilli leaned close to Zack. "Looks like Drambetsky is granting us some private time with Frank."

Frank Culhane fumbled with the screen door, which slapped shut behind him. He moved away from the officer guarding him and stepped onto the porch. Dark half-moons cupped his eyes. Zack shook hands with him and introduced Lilli.

"Morning, ma'am," Frank said wearily and touched the brim of his cowboy hat. "Thanks for coming," he said to Zack. "You always were a fair player on the court. That's more than I know about the FBI agents."

Agent Drambetsky coughed and then shook the porch railing as if testing for termite damage.

Frank dug his hands into his pockets. "Lobo says you can help me, Zack. I couldn't tell him what a mess I've made of things. It's easier to tell you than my future brother-in-law that I'm a jerk."

"Take it easy," Zack said. "I hear from Lobo that you're a decent guy."

"Let's go over there." Frank led Zack and Lilli to

a wooden picnic table and chairs beneath a towering cypress tree. Zack signaled to Drambetsky that everything was okay. "Agent Drambetsky thinks I'm a fool and—"

A commotion coming from the barn interrupted Frank. Lilli looked up and saw the FBI agents ushering the immigrants toward waiting vans. Several clung to the barn door and had to be led away. "Stay. Let us stay," a small hunched-over man called out in English. "Please, Frank! You good man!" He reached out his hands toward Frank, pleading. "Tell them. Let us stay!"

"Go have a look at how they lived," Frank said, lowering his head, "and see if you still think I'm a decent person. They made so little money from poaching that they could hardly afford food."

"That wasn't your fault," Zack said.

Frank gnawed at the inside of his cheek. "I did my best by them, but it was never enough. The whole thing turned my stomach. They took home scraps of food from the restaurants where they worked and cooked soup in my barn. That's how they survived. Pitiful. Just plain pitiful."

"Surely the restaurants fed them," Lilli said.

"Yes, but the immigrants only worked during dinner rush hours and ate only one meal. In the morning before the sun got too hot they worked the fields picking crops. I was forced to fire my regular crew and hire them. By the time I paid protection for me and them, there was hardly any money left. My skin just crawls telling you about their crummy life and knowing I was partly to blame."

Lilli sat down next to Frank. "I still can't believe that none of the restaurant owners took pity on the immigrants."

"You can thank Bulldog for that."

Zack gulped. "Bulldog?"

"Bulldog hinted that he was about to be promoted by his 'boss lady.' That's what he called Madame Kwan. 'No more terrorizing poachers in crummy parks at night,' Bulldog said. He bragged that soon he'd be eating real meals in nice restaurants."

"What do you suppose Bulldog meant?" Zack asked.

Frank shrugged. "I never asked any questions, but he let slip that his new job would involved VOCRA."

"VOCRA, The Volusia County Restaurant Association," Lilli said, thinking out loud. "Mrs. D'Amato's cousin Luigi and other VOCRA people are meeting at the Paradisio Suites today. That's where—"

"Madame Kwan is staying," Zack finished her sentence.

"What a nice little coincidence." Lilli smiled. "Let's tell Drambetsky."

"There's time for that later," Zack said and looked directly at Frank. "Let's see what we can do to finish up here so you can go see your girls."

Lilli sensed that although the VOCRA connection

was important, Zack didn't want to call in Drambetsky and lose his momentum with Frank. But what more could he possibly hope to draw out of Frank Culhane?

TWENTY

The Sentimental Heart

FRANK GRIPPED THE EDGE of the picnic table and leaned forward. "My girls are scared. They lost their mother. They're afraid of losing me. I could be locked up for a real long time."

"That's not certain," Zack said. "There's no denying you harbored illegal immigrants and were involved in transporting them to poaching sites. But if you cooperate, the jury will probably take that into consideration and go easy on you."

"I've told the FBI all I know," Frank said, his voice agitated. "I want to help, but I can't concentrate. All I can think about are my girls."

"Lobo tells me your girls are terrific," Zack said and Frank's face lit up. "If you're the wonderful father Lobo says, I'm sure you have some photos handy."

"Sure do." Frank whipped out his wallet and flashed a photo at Zack and Lilli. "Here's my big girl, Laurie, and her baby sister, Emma. That's Consuela in the middle." Two girls with blond pigtails and matching outfits sat on a seesaw. Emma, her feet planted on the ground, waved at the camera. Laurie, riding high, her feet stretched out to either side, rewarded the photographer with a fearless expression. Consuela, with a strong family resemblance to Lobo, smiled into the bright sunshine and held out her arms as if to embrace both girls.

"Beautiful girls," Lilli commented.

"They had a beautiful mother," Frank replied. He looked up at Zack. "I know you're trying to get me to relax, talking about my girls and all, but we'd better get to your questions."

"Right," Zack said and slid the photo toward Frank. "Did Jackal ever talk much about his 'boss lady,' Madame Kwan?"

"Jackal said she'd arrange things so that I'd be declared an unfit parent and that my kids would be taken away." Frank's voice wavered. "I went along with whatever Jackal and his boss lady wanted. I didn't have a choice, at least that's the way I saw it."

Lilli thought her heart would break, seeing the desperation in Frank's eyes.

Frank picked at the table's splintered wood. "I can't wait for this to be over. All I want is to settle down with my girls and Consuela and get a decent life going."

"Sounds like a good plan." Zack leaned forward and a determined expression crossed his face. "Let's talk some more about Jackal. Is there anything you might have forgotten to tell the FBI agents?"

"I told them everything I know."

"Did Jackal ever tell you anything personal, you know, let slip something about himself, like the name of some friends, something like that. Take your time. Think about all your conversations."

"That won't take long. Jackal grunted and did most of his talking with his hands."

"Think," Zack said. "Something will come to mind."

Frank rested his head in his hands. Zack looked at Lilli and shrugged as if to say 'I don't think he has anything to tell us.'

Frank shook his head. "Nothing's jumping out at me. All I can see is his big meaty hands, adjusting that brand-new belt with the shiny buckle."

"A *silver* buckle?" Zack and Lilli both asked.

"Yes," Frank said, obviously surprised that they knew it was silver. "There was some kind of animal head on the buckle. I asked him about it once. He bragged that it was a gift from his boss lady for 'special' work he'd done for her. He didn't come out and say so, but I guessed he meant he'd killed someone to earn that belt. He said it came from some special store in Chinatown."

"Do you know the name of the store?" Zack asked.

"I can't remember it," Frank said, "but I think I'd know it if I heard it."

"What did it sound like? Was it Pearl Street? Paine Street? Park? Elizabeth? Mott Street?" Zack hammered away with questions.

"Mott. Not Mott. But maybe something with an M." Frank shrugged. "I don't know. I've never been to

New York City or Chinatown. I'm drawing a big blank. Sorry."

"M-A. M-E. M-O." Lilli rattled off the letters, trying to be helpful.

Zack signaled Lilli to move away as if her presence threatened Frank, as if he were being ganged up on. Well, Zack was the one badgering Frank with questions, not her.

Fuming, Lilli got up, moved a few feet away, and leaned against the trunk of the cypress tree. She crossed her arms over her chest and glared at Zack. A piece of bark scraped her arm. She moved, but it still tore at her skin. Scowling, she turned and looked at the tree. Near her shoulder, someone had carved a heart pierced by an arrow. The initials FC and CC were linked with an addition sign. She figured that the carving, not yet dark with age, was quite recent.

"Frank Culhane and Consuela Cruz," Lilli murmured, running her fingertips over the carved letters. How sentimental, she thought, for a couple to declare their love in such an old-fashioned way.

"That's me and Consuela's names on that cypress tree," Frank exclaimed and turned beet red at his sudden outburst. "Hey, wait a minute," he said. "Tree. The store where the belt came from was on a street named after a tree."

"Are you sure?" Zack asked.

"Yeah. I remember him making a joke about a tree and him, a jungle animal, a jackal."

"A tree. Good, that's a start," Zack said encouragingly.

"A tree in Chinatown," Lilli added. "And it starts with the letter M."

Zack snapped his fingers. "Mulberry Street!"

"Mulberry. That's it," Frank said. "The store that sent his belt was on Mulberry Street."

Zack's jaw dropped. "Did you say the store *sent* it?"

"That's what Jackal told me."

"This could be the break we've been hoping for," Zack said. "I'll let Agent Drambetsky know. If that store shipped belts for Madame Kwan, then we have the names of her killer squad. I'd wager that at least one of them will cut a deal and Madame Kwan will face charges of conspiracy to commit murder. So far, we know the body in the midden mound and the body in New York City had those belt buckles. Now Jackal, too. My boss has been tracking down shops, but this narrows the list." Zack's eyes glistened. "Madame Kwan done in by her own generosity. She'll go ballistic when she finds out."

"I wouldn't want to be close to her sleeves and those hidden knives when she does," Lilli said. Her green eyes sparkled like emeralds. "Hey, Zack, don't forget. The guy in Tomoka Park with the orchid tattoo wore a fancy silver clip on his ponytail. Your boss should check on silver buckles *and* silver clips."

"A photographer's eyes are even sharper than a

detective's," Zack said, obviously proud of Lilli. "Good going," Zack said, shaking hands with Frank. "Your information could be just what the FBI wants." Zack waved to Agent Drambetsky, smiled broadly, and then turned to Lilli. "And thanks for your help, too."

Lilli nudged Zack playfully. "Hey, we're a team, remember?"

Drambetsky and the agent who had been guarding Frank strode toward the picnic bench. Zack filled them in on Madame Kwan's 'gift list' of hired killers and her interest in VOCRA. "The VOCRA members are meeting at the Paradisio Suites today," Zack said and checked his watch. "Madame Kwan was due to check in not long ago. We need to find out what she's up to."

Drambetsky said, "I'll call the agents at the Paradisio and alert them to the VOCRA situation. This puts a new wrinkle on Madame Kwan's choice of hotels. As soon as we finish up here, I'll head over there myself." He turned to Frank. "Your cooperation will definitely work for you when Madame Kwan comes to trial. Count on it. As for you," he nodded to Lilli and Zack. "I leaned on you real hard, but I got the results I wanted."

"Is that part of the FBI training in personal relations?" Zack asked.

"Nah. It's my own special style." Agent Drambetsky sliced his fingers across his throat. "I go straight for the jugular." He shook hands with Frank and sent him along to the barn with the other FBI agent. Lilli thought

Frank walked taller, as if a tremendous weight had been removed from his shoulders.

Agent Drambetsky chuckled. "Hey, Lilli, see how nice I was to Frank? I'm not a hard-nosed bully, like you think. Not when it comes to immigrants."

"You're a real sweetheart," Lilli snapped.

"Cut me some slack," Agent Drambetsky said. "My grandparents came over from the Old Country on an immigrant 'coffin ship.' They were lucky to survive the diseases and filthy conditions below deck. They told me stories about the sweatshops and tenements they endured in America and the creeps who preyed on them, squeezing out their last pennies. Every time I can put someone like Madame Kwan behind bars, I feel it's a victory for my grandparents. They've been dead for years, but it's never too late to make amends."

Drambetsky waved away his emotional words. "Don't either of you start thinking you're indispensable to this case, but I'd like you both to stick around." He pointed at the immigrants who were stepping out of the vans. "We've decided to ease up. We'll take off the handcuffs and question them here instead of at police headquarters."

"Good idea," Zack said.

Lilli smiled. "You have some redeeming qualities after all."

"Don't get getting all warm and fuzzy on me, Lilli," Agent Drambetsky said. "I'm just doing my job. Here, in familiar surroundings and with Frank's

encouragement—which I think we can count on now—
the immigrants might spill their guts about Kwan. I'd
bet at least one of them was an eyewitness to a murder
or knows somebody who was."

"Before we head over to the barn," Zack said, "I'd like
to call Lobo and tell him how helpful Frank was."

"Sure. Just don't go telling Lobo that I have a heart.
That kind of stuff gets a guy a bad reputation in this
business."

As Agent Drambetsky walked toward the barn, Zack
called Lobo. Sitting down at the picnic table, Lilli saw
Zack smile and figured that he and Lobo were patch-
ing up their quarrel. As their conversation continued,
she watched the immigrants gathering around Frank.
Body language told her that the FBI agents and interpreters were allowing Frank to set the pace and run
the show. Judging by the immigrants' karate chops and
pantomime stabbings, followed by falling down and
playing-dead routines, they were acting out Madame
Kwan's viciousness.

Lilli wished there was something she could do to
help put Madame Kwan in prison for life. But what?
She reached into her tote bag for a tissue and her hand
touched the Bouquet of Roses cologne. She remembered
that Madame Kwan was allergic to roses. How ironic,
she thought, that a delicate rose, the symbol of love, had
power over the hateful and mighty Madame Kwan. Lilli
was about to spray her wrists when she heard Zack say
goodbye to Lobo.

"What's up?" Lilli asked.

"Lobo told me the FBI set up surveillance cameras at the Paradisio Suites. They finished just before Madame Kwan and her entourage of bodyguards checked in this morning." Zack chuckled. "I'm told it was quite a production."

"Hidden cameras, taps on her phones, bugs hidden in her light fixtures. Stuff like that?" Lilli asked.

"Heck no. I'm talking about Madame Kwan and her bodyguards and their big movie-star entrance. Try to imagine an army of women in dark glasses, slinky dresses, spiky heels." He laughed heartily. "Lots of leg and cleavage. According to Lobo, the FBI agents got a real eyeful. Wish I—"

Zack cut himself off, but Lilli knew he wished he'd been there. She stretched her legs, wiggling the toes of her hiking boots, tightening her calf and thigh muscles. Why didn't Zack look at *her* legs? They were her best feature. In junior high she had been "gangly." By high school, she'd graduated to "athletic." In college, she was "that leggy redhead."

"Come on." Zack pulled Lilli to her feet. "Looks like you have cramps in both legs. Walking's the best thing for it. Let's go talk Drambetsky into letting us go to the Paradisio Suites. I'd like to check out Madame Kwan's connection to VOCRA."

"Why don't you tell Drambetsky that you know Chef Luigi and could ferret out information from him about VOCRA? The Faraday charm worked with Frank

Culhane. It could work again with Luigi. Maybe it could even captivate Madame Kwan."

Zack cocked his eyebrow as if contemplating her idea. Lilli was already imagining herself meeting the infamous Madame Kwan and laughing as the dark-haired beauty was hauled away in handcuffs, accused of heinous crimes against humanity. Then she thought about Zack coming under Madame Kwan's spell and falling for her seductive appeal. Grrr!

TWENTY-ONE

By Invitation Only

"I FELT SORRY FOR EVERYONE at Frank's place—the immigrants, Frank and the agents," Lilli said as she and Zack pulled into Kate's driveway. "Madame Kwan is the most despicable person I've ever heard of. I wish we could go to the Paradisio Suites and help the FBI get more evidence against her."

"You heard Agent Drambetsky," Zack said.

Lilli nodded. "His 'no, absolutely not, over my dead body' sounded final."

Mrs. D'Amato came running toward the car, waving an envelope with tickets poking out of it. "I have such good news," she greeted Lilli and Zack. "Someone named Agent Drambetsky called and said that both of you are going to accompany me to the VOCRA Convention at the Paradisio Suites. Lobo, too. I hated the thought of going alone. And now…why, this is so unexpected!"

"Drambetsky changed his mind," Lilli exclaimed. "I can't believe it."

"There is one small glitch," Mrs. D'Amato said. "Agent Drambetsky is expecting a call from you, Lilli.

He wants to—what was his word?—'clarify' your role before he'll let any of us go." She wagged her finger at Lilli. "Please don't spoil my big day…or Luigi's."

Lilli jumped out of the car and slammed the door. "Drambetsky is a control freak." She kicked the front tire. "Did he forget I helped crack this case? That should entitle me to go, too!"

"Calm down, Lilli," Zack said and then turned to Mrs. D'Amato. "What exactly did Drambetsky say?"

"He said Lobo would explain," Mrs. D'Amato replied, "but he'll have to tell us later. We need to get ready. You'll want to watch Luigi prepare his mussels marinara. And then, you can listen to my latest repertoire of love songs. That will be the frosting on the cake…or should I say, on the mussels marinara."

Mrs. D'Amato trilled a few notes. "Lucky for you there were some last-minute cancellations and Luigi scooped up the tickets. Can you believe our good fortune? It's by invitation only." She kissed the envelope. "I wanted Kate to go, but John says it's too dangerous with Madame Kwan and her bodyguard roaming around. He and Kate will stay home, and they seem happy about it." She lowered her voice. "John says the Paradisio will be swarming with FBI and we're in no real danger…as long as Lilli sticks to the FBI's plan."

"Hold it!" Lilli sputtered.

Mrs. D'Amato plowed on. "Don't worry, John and Lobo swore me to secrecy. I didn't let on to Luigi about the FBI being at the Paradisio. Besides, I didn't want to make his head swell with pride. His mussels marinara recipe is great, but guarding it is hardly a matter of national security!" She spun on her heel and her skirt swirled around her ankles. "We should dress real nice."

Zack laughed. "For you, Mrs. D'Amato, that means two boas instead of one!"

Mrs. D'Amato hurried toward her front door. "Be ready in thirty minutes," she called over her shoulder.

LOBO LOOKED UP FROM the living room window where he was tightening the locks. "You heard Drambetsky changed his mind? We can go."

"We?" Lilli snapped.

Lobo gave the screwdriver a final turn. "Drambetsky says you're impulsive, Lilli. He's afraid you'll ruin the FBI's chance to get that little black book away from Madame Kwan."

Lilli fumed. "How come he's letting the rest of you go?"

"I can't wait to hear this," Zack said.

"I didn't want the FBI to have all the glory," Lobo said. "It's only right that a local detective—like me, for instance—should be there. And since you helped my future brother-in-law, I figure you earned a place there, too."

"I'll bet that's not how you phrased it," Zack said.

Lobo grinned. "I told Drambetsky that Luigi would be suspicious if Mrs. D'Amato didn't bring guests. Luigi is, after all, an award-winning chef and certainly his family, friends and fans would attend." Lobo chose a smaller screwdriver from his toolbox. "And I reminded Drambetsky that Luigi might mention it to the other VOCRA chefs. You know how word travels, I told Drambetsky. If, as we suspect, Madame Kwan is involved with VOCRA, she'd hear, get suspicious about why people were avoiding the event and she might back off. We don't want to tip her off that she and VOCRA are under surveillance. We want to see what she's up to, that's the idea I hammered home with Drambetsky. He bought it and said we could go. Then he hedged and said Lilli needed to promise him something."

Lilli sighed. "Spell it out."

"You must promise to remain in the background."

"No problem," Lilli said, gritting her teeth.

Lobo traded his screwdriver for a hammer. "Lilli, you are there as Mrs. D'Amato's friend, as Luigi's fan, as Zack's girlfriend, whatever…but not as a detective, a role Drambetsky claims you relish."

"I understand," Lilli said sweetly, honey practically dripping from her lips.

Lobo cocked his eyebrow. "You're window dressing, Lilli. Drambetsky's allowing you to go just to make the scene believable to anyone who might be suspicious."

"I'd better call Drambetsky," Lilli said.

Lobo punched in numbers and handed Lilli the phone. "Don't get creative," he warned.

"Behave yourself," Zack added.

"Agent Drambetsky," Lilli purred and then jerked

the phone away as Drambetsky's voice blasted into the room. "Of course, sir. That's how I see it, too." She forced a sickly sweet smile. "I'm a team player and you're the captain. You can count on my full cooperation." There was a pause and Lilli pretended to toss a football. "Thank you for being such a good sport," she said and hung up.

"There, that wasn't so difficult, was it?" Zack asked.

Lilli's frosty glance gave way to a smile. "Drambetsky is a real sweetheart."

Zack chuckled. "Hey, Lobo, about those VOCRA invitations conveniently showing up—"

"All in a day's work," Lobo said and moved on to the next window. "Oh, Zack, I almost forgot. Your boss called and left a message. They located the shop that sold Madame Kwan the special-order silver merchandise. It's Metals Exotica, on Mulberry Street, in Chinatown. So now we have the names of Madame Kwan's killer squadron."

"Did my boss say anything else?" Zack asked warily and drained the glass.

"Yes. He's been in touch with the FBI and the Ormond Police. You're back in his good graces, whatever that means."

"It means I have a job when I go back to the precinct," Zack said.

Lilli thought he smiled like a kid discovering a shiny new bike on Christmas morning. "I'm glad everything's working out for you," she said reassuringly.

He kissed her lightly on the cheek. "You bring me good luck," he said.

Kate steered herself into the living room from her studio. "Lilli, I hear you're going to the restaurant convention. Did you bring something suitable for an afternoon gala at a fancy hotel?'

"The usual little black dress. Boring, but it will have to do."

"We can do better. Follow me," Kate said, rolling into her bedroom, located off the living room. She opened her closet and Lilli couldn't believe the rows of beautiful skirts, blouses and dresses.

"Pick what you'd like," Kate said, "but this green suit would look fabulous on you." She ruffled the long silk skirt hanging next to the matching jacket with a row of tiny buttons that sparkled like diamonds. "Try it on. It's perfect for you."

Lilli held up the outfit, which played up her green eyes and pale skin. "It's beautiful," she said, looking at her reflection in the mirror, "but it's brand new. I couldn't."

"I insist," Kate said. "Try it on," she said, opening the door to her bathroom and dressing area.

Lilli objected halfheartedly, knowing that the clingy bias-cut skirt would complement her slim figure. While Lilli slipped into the suit, Kate chatted away, making small talk. Then Kate's voice turned serious. "I called my parents and we had a heart-to-heart about the accident. They need some time to come to grips with the guilt I piled on them, but I'm hoping they'll understand."

There was a long silence and finally Kate said, "Do you think Zack will ever forgive me?"

"He already has," Lilli said, returning to the bedroom.

"You look gorgeous," Kate said, "and I have just the shoes to go with that suit."

"It's probably none of my business," Lilli said, sitting on Kate's bed, "but you did a very brave thing admitting what really happened the day of your accident."

"Honest, not brave."

"Both," Lilli conceded. "And as long as I'm offering my opinion, I don't believe Ted was ever worthy of you."

"Thanks. I'm going to try and get in touch with the truck driver…but not Ted. Let Ted suffer. I'm allowing myself some anger and meanness." She laughed. "Enough of this. The shoes are still in the box up there on the shelf."

"I'll get them," Lilli said, but Kate beat her to it, and gripped the shoebox with a long-handled claw that hung outside her closet.

Lilli couldn't believe the shoes. Green silk sandals with three-inch spike heels.

"I know what you're thinking," Kate said. "But if I'm only going to sit and look at my shoes, what the heck, let them be glamorous. All of my fancy shoes are like that."

Lilli took a few steps and felt as if she were about to fall off a mountain. She saw the look of eager expectation on Kate's face. "They're perfect," she said, gripping the bureau to steady herself.

"Let's get Zack's opinion," Kate said, calling to him.

Zack rushed into Kate's bedroom, looking handsome in his dark conservative suit and striped tie. "Is there a problem?" he asked, and then he saw Lilli. "Wow! You look...tall," he said.

"It's the shoes." Lilli wobbled toward Zack. She was five feet seven inches tall, but began to appreciate how the world looked to professional basketball players.

"Well, for once we see eye to eye," he said and then kissed her on the cheek. "You are a knockout," he complimented and retreated from the room, looking at her shoes and shaking his head in amazement.

"Promise me something," Kate said when Zack was gone.

"Name it."

"Promise you'll kick up your heels for both of us."

TWENTY-TWO

The Paradisio Suites Hotel

THE HEELS OF LILLI'S SHOES sank into the Paradisio Suite's plush white carpet as she stood with Zack near the bank of elevators on the second floor. The hallways of the second through fifth floors formed balconies open to the lobby below, lending the glamorous hotel an open, airy feeling. Lilli ran her fingertips along the white marble banister of the winding staircase that swept dramatically to the lobby. Craning her neck, she admired the twelve massive gold-trimmed chandeliers suspended from the ceiling three floors above. The crystal teardrop prisms glistened in the late-afternoon light filtering through the slender windows that pierced the hotel's golden walls.

Directly below, near the registration area, a pianist wearing a white tuxedo played romantic melodies on a white baby grand. A pond with a gurgling waterfall and wind chimes dangling between potted palms enhanced the illusion of serenity. Lobo and several FBI agents that Lilli recognized from Frank's home strolled among the guests. Lilli's attention was drawn to the swooshing sound from the elevators, which stopped and emptied their guests into the crowd. Many clutched programs for the restaurateurs' convention, which was taking place in the Grand Pavilion at the rear of the lobby.

"Remember our plan," Zack was saying. "First, we let Luigi cook and Mrs. D'Amato sing. Then we'll see what Luigi and his friends can tell us about Madame Kwan's ties to VOCRA, their restaurant association. Maybe they know something about her little black book, too. I'm convinced that's the evidence that will seal her fate."

Lilli sighed. "Our plan is so simple, how could I forget it?" She sighed again. "While we wait for Luigi, let's ride the express elevator to the Starlight Lounge. We can check out the view of Daytona Beach."

"I thought you wanted to try out the staircase," Zack said. "What the heck. We have time for both before Luigi and Mrs. D'Amato perform."

"According to Mrs. D'Amato, they plan to synchronize her operatic artistry and his culinary expertise."

"Synchronize?" Zack laughed. "They'll both try to steal the show." He hooked his arm through Lilli's. "Let's go. There's the express elevator."

"It's too crowded," Lilli said, backing away, feeling a tinge of claustrophobia. "Let's wait for the next one."

"We might run into Madame Kwan and her bodyguards," Zack said. "Promise me you won't get any funny ideas. Remember there are hidden cameras everywhere and the FBI is watching. One wrong move, and they'll pull you out of here."

Lilli tugged at Zack's sleeve. "I must confess I've

got an idea how we can get into Madame Kwan's room and steal her little black book. I've seen it done in lots of movies. It always works."

"We don't have time for your crazy schemes," Zack said.

"Could you just listen?"

Zack groaned, resigned to his fate.

"We disguise ourselves as a waiter and waitress. We knock on Madame Kwan's door. 'Dinner is served madame,' I announce with my best French 101 accent, and you roll in a service cart that contains Madame Kwan's fancy dinner. It's probably roast pig with an apple stuck in its mouth. That's the usual choice." The words tumbled from Lilli's lips as she waited for the elevator. "Once inside, you pull back the tablecloth and reach for the gun which you buried in the napkins. You poke it in the surprised faces of Madame Kwan and her bodyguards and tell them to hand over the little black book. If they resist, I grab the alligator purse and run for it. You quickly pull on your gas mask, toss your canister of sleeping potion into the center of the room, and back out the doorway." She chuckled. "You have my permission to laugh triumphantly as everyone falls to the carpet already fast asleep."

"Let's take a second look at the scene," Zack said calmly. "We enter. Hee-yah! Hee-yah!" He karate-chopped left, then right. "The hellcats jump us and do their dirty work while Madame Kwan laughs—triumphantly of course—at our amateurish invasion. Before we know what hit us, we'll be rolling down the corridor on the service cart, tied up with apples poking out of our mouths."

"Zack, you're such a spoilsport. You take all the fun out of my ideas."

Zack put his arm around her waist. "You seem to have forgotten that we're here to obtain information from Luigi. The FBI agents will take care of Madame Kwan."

Lilli pouted. "And their plan is better than mine?"

"Let's just say their plan is in the, uh, formative stages. They hope to take Madame Kwan's book and copy it without her being aware it's missing. If you figure out how to do that, let me know. The entire FBI, as well as the combined Ormond Beach and New York City Police Department, will be forever in your debt."

Zack checked his watch. "Wait right here while I make a quick call to my boss." He took off, smiling at Lilli and shaking his head.

For gosh sake! He treated her like a starry-eyed movie fan who deluded herself with visions of bringing down Madame Kwan's entire operation. Well, maybe she could. Lilli squared her shoulders. And maybe she would!

Lilli considered slipping into a maid's uniform and entering Madame Kwan's suite. If all went smoothly like in the movies, Madame Kwan would be in the shower. As steam swirled from the bathroom into the living room and Madame Kwan warbled an exotic song, Lilli

would plump the couch pillows and, seizing the oppor-
tune moment, slip a sleeping potion into the teacups of
the two bodyguards. They would slink to the floor and
fall asleep, curled up like little kitten dolls in silk paja-
mas. Lilli would slither into the bedroom, open Madame
Kwan's alligator purse and remove the little black book.
As she closed the suite door silently behind her, she
would hear the water running in the shower, Madame
Kwan warbling and the bodyguards snoring softly.

What a great spy movie! She, Lilli, the heroine, had
foiled Madame Kwan, the villain. Goodness conquered
evil. All was right with the world. Lilli reached into her
tote bag and pulled out her Bouquet of Roses cologne.
She boldly depressed the atomizer several times and
directed the mist to her wrists and neck. Whew! The
fragrance was more pungent than she remembered.

Lilli stepped away from the strong scent that tickled
her nose and made her eyes water. She gripped the banister to steady herself on her wobbly heels. Blinking away
the stinging sensation, she watched the people exiting
from the elevator. Like the previous groups, they milled
around and then holding their chins high like kings and
queens, descended the staircase. Lilli teetered forward
and wondered what kind of shoes Scarlett O'Hara wore
when she floated down the stairs into Rhett Butler's
arms. Several more elevators emptied their guests.

Lilli looked down at the lobby and saw Zack leaning against the baby grand and talking to the pianist.
Suddenly Zack reached across an island of phones and

picked up the receiver the moment someone set it down. So that's what was taking him so long. The phones were busy.

Swoosh! The doors of the elevator nearest the staircase opened. A smattering of Chinese words struck Lilli's ears. She peered past the shoulders and heads of the crowd. Madame Kwan, two of her bodyguards and several guests stepped out of the elevator. Madame Kwan was coming her way. Ducking down, hoping not to be seen, Lilli squirted the Bouquet of Roses cologne at herself. *Spht!* She prayed her neck. *Spht! Spht!* She sprayed her wrists. Madame Kwan sneezed. Lilli sprayed again and again.

Madame Kwan doubled over in a fit of sneezes and mumbled something in Chinese. Her bodyguards jumped into attack mode, knees bent, arms stretched out, their hands flattened and circling as if to strike. Their feet moved forward and back, prepared to spring in any direction. Their suspicious eyes took in the crowd, looking for potential troublemakers. Lilli was sure they were looking straight at her.

Madame Kwan regained her composure. "Out of my way," she bellowed at the hotel guests blocking her way to the stairs. She snapped open her alligator purse, pulled out a handkerchief, and wiped the tears from her eyes. Lilli barged ahead, pulling a camera from her tote bag with one hand and squirting cologne with the other.

Madame Kwan stamped her feet. Unable to catch her

breath or speak because of the rapid-fire sneezes, she made big sweeping motions with her hands. She pointed in Lilli's direction as if trying to alert her bodyguards to the source of her distress.

Lilli bumped into Madame Kwan as hard as she could. Madame Kwan's wide-open purse spewed its contents. The black book landed near Lilli's feet. "Excuse me. New shoes…tricky heels…slippery soles. I'm so sorry." Lilli apologized profusely for her awkwardness as she teetered and tottered.

Madame Kwan blew her nose and continued sneezing while trying to avoid Lilli, who was tottering toward her with the cologne bottle. Lilli reached out and grabbed hold of the bodyguards' shoulders. "Sorry! I'm so sorry!" she said, tripping and pulling them to the floor with her. She cocked her knee and kicked with all her might. She caught Madame Kwan's book with the sole of her shoe and sent the ribbon-wrapped missile in between two of the banister's spindles.

Lilli heard the chandelier prisms tinkle, followed by several discordant notes from the piano. She knew immediately the route the little black book had taken. Praying that she wouldn't hear a splash in the pond, she pulled herself to her feet. She was just in time to see Zack peer into the piano and retrieve the book.

Lilli imagined Zack dashing into the men's room and furiously photographing page after page. But this would take much longer than the twelve pages he had photographed in Bulldog's motor home. Lilli had to keep Madame Kwan and the bodyguards away from the lobby, away from Zack. But how? Of course! She pitched forward and fell, dumping the contents of her tote bag onto the carpet.

"Hey! Watch it! These are expensive cameras," Lilli exclaimed to the crowd that had gathered. She began picking up her cameras, film and supplies. Pointing at Lilli, the bodyguards screamed words that Lilli couldn't understand, but she knew threats when she heard them. She grabbed her tote bag and tottered toward the elevators. The bodyguards, who were shrieking and clearing a path by executing karate chops and kicks with laser speed, blocked her way.

"This is a stunt!" a man in the crowd hooted. "It must be an advertisement for the Chinese food demonstration downstairs." Many in the crowd nodded agreement and formed a large circle so that they could see the action. Eyes blazing, the shorter bodyguard rushed at Lilli. Lilli dove onto the carpet and rolled toward the circle of gawking guests, hoping to break through and get away. Awed, the crowd didn't break ranks.

"Please, help me," Lilli pleaded, rising onto her knees.

"She must be a professional wrestler," a woman with curly black hair said.

A woman wearing a red dress added, "She won't win in those shoes."

Finally the taller bodyguard came up behind Lilli, grabbed her under the arms, and dragged her toward the elevator. Lilli kicked and screamed. Startled, she recognized FBI Agent Douglas Drambetsky in the crowd.

"Let's make this a fair fight," Agent Drambetsky exclaimed and yanked the bodyguard away from Lilli. He leaned close and whispered, "You've gone this far. Keep it up for one more minute." He leaned back and shoved away the other bodyguard.

Madame Kwan wiped her eyes. "Where is my book?" she screeched in heavily accented English, venom practically dripping from her lips. Between fits of sneezing, Madame Kwan sunk her fingernails into Lilli's upper arm. "You stole my little black book."

"I did not," Lilli said haughtily, towering over Madame Kwan. "I've got my own little black book, full of men's names. More men than I can handle. You've heard the expression, so little time, so many men. That's the story of my life, ha ha." Lilli noticed that Madame Kwan wasn't laughing. Tears streamed from her red and swollen eyes. "What would I want with your men? Mine are a lot younger than yours, ha ha!"

Lilli saw a flash of red nails and her cheek stung.

"Is there a problem?" asked a pudgy man in gold and cream uniform bustling toward Madame Kwan and Lilli. Madame Kwan struggled to control her sneezing and coughing.

"Yes there is," Madame Kwan sputtered, pointing at Lilli. "This despicable creature stole my book." She coughed. "It's a treasured family heirloom with sen-

timental value." She sneezed. "I want it back right now."
She sneezed again. "Search her immediately!"

The security guard shrugged. "Please, madame,
speak more slowly. I can't understand you."

"Find it!" Madame Kwan bellowed, jabbing his epaulettes with her index finger and backing him into the
wall. "Find my little black book." She sneezed. "It's
unique." She sneezed again. "It has ribbons around
it."

"Oh *that* book," he said. "Well, then, my dear lady,
the problem is solved. It landed in the lobby several
minutes ago. We couldn't read Chinese so we couldn't
tell to whom it belonged. We took it to Lost and Found.
Please follow me, fill out a few forms as required by
Paradisio Suite's policy, and we will gladly return it to
you." He turned on his heel and proceeded to the staircase. Agent Drambetsky and several men in dark suits
followed him.

Madame Kwan shot Lilli a look that would curdle
milk. Flanked by her bodyguards, she marched down
the stairs. The chopstick-shaped hair ornaments, once
neatly crisscrossed through her upswept hair, now dangled to her collar, clacking with every step she took.

Another employee dressed in cream and gold ap-
proached Lilli. "An important call for you, miss," he
said and presented a white telephone resting on a golden
velvet pillow.

"Hello?" Lilli said, trying to free the heels of her
shoes, which were caught in the hem of her skirt.

"Lilli, this is Zack. If you're all done with your aerobic workout, I was wondering if you'd like to accompany me to the Grand Pavilion. I'm working up an appetite. How about some mussels marinara?"

"Great," Lilli said. "Anything…except chop suey."

She tossed her shoes in her tote bag, scooped up the droopy hem of her skirt, and trotted down the stairs. She hoped her trembling knees didn't give in. She saw Madame Kwan at the Lost and Found counter, alternately tapping her nails on the counter and jabbing them at the attendant's epaulettes.

Zack rushed toward Lilli. "You were incredible," he whispered. "Your little performance gave the FBI enough time to copy the entire book. They were ready to step in if necessary, but you had everything under control."

A disappointed look crossed her face. "You didn't race into the men's room and copy the book with your camera?"

"Are you kidding? The FBI zapped it with their high-tech equipment. I was busy convincing the pianist that a small black shoe had fallen and struck his piano. I told him it's an old Chinese custom meant to bring good luck."

"Did he believe you?" Lilli asked.

"I think so. He's planning on wearing a biker's helmet until the restaurateurs' convention is over." Zack backed away, pinching his nose. "What kind of perfume is that?"

"Bouquet of Roses," she said. "Be sure to thank Digger. It did the trick."

Zack held Lilli at arm's length. "You look so, uh, short. Madame Kwan and her hellcats must have cut you down to size."

Lilli tried to jab Zack but he wrapped his arms around her and drew her close. He kissed her long and hard right there in the middle of the lobby. "Thanks for all your help," he whispered, holding her tight. "But don't do anything that foolish again. I've gotten used to having you around."

Coming from Zack, that was the equivalent of 'I hope to share the rest of my life with you.' "Don't worry," she said, "I'm not going anywhere without you."

Agent Drambetsky rushed through the crowd of visitors to Lilli's side. "You're leaving right now and you're coming with us, Faraday," he said brusquely, escorting them toward a side door marked Employees Only.

"What's happened?" Zack asked, looking over his shoulder, his voice tense.

Agent Drambetsky pushed open the door and hurried Lilli and Zack down a long winding corridor. "Madame Kwan is suspicious about her precious book being out of her hands for even a few minutes. She's hissing and carrying on, looking for...this is a direct quote...'a crazy redhead wearing skyscraper shoes.' She says the redhead humiliated her. She's threatening revenge. Lilli, I thought you understood you weren't to jump into the middle of things. You were terrific, but you could have ruined everything."

"Thanks for the, uh, compliment," Lilli mumbled.

They exited through a doorway into an alley that led to a service road and the highway beyond. Lilli noticed a dark car with tinted windows approaching slowly, its lights blinking.

"Lilli, you're going to Kate's immediately," Agent Drambetsky said. "You're in extreme danger here."

"No," Lilli objected.

"Do what Agent Drambetsky says," Zack insisted, putting his arm protectively across her shoulders.

Agent Drambetsky opened the car door. "Here's more bad news. Bulldog slipped by us and he's on the loose. We've sent an Ormond Beach Officer to help John protect you and Kate. You're safer at Kate's than here."

"Go on, Lilli," Zack said, putting his hand on the car door.

Lilli didn't object. The concern in Zack's eyes frightened her. He closed the car door and the driver sped toward the service road. When Lilli looked back, Zack and Drambetsky were running down the alley toward the Paradisio Suites. She prayed that Madame Kwan wouldn't take out her revenge on them.

TWENTY-THREE

Staying Alive

"LILLI," KATE CALLED UP to the loft, "phone call for you. It's Zack on the secure line."

Lilli jumped up, spilling the pages of text she'd been writing, and rushed downstairs. It was eight o'clock and this was the first she'd heard from Zack since she'd left the Paradisio Suites. That was hours ago. To calm her frayed nerves, she'd been working on her biker article for *Viewpoint* magazine. Kate, John and Officer Grady were tense, too, as if they expected Bulldog to burst in at any minute, but they put up a cheerful front. Sort of like whistling in the dark, Lilli thought, but she'd gone along hoping to ease everyone's fears, including her own.

"How's everything?" Zack asked.

"Fine." She didn't want to admit that she jumped at every sound and saw Bulldog's face at every window. Zack had enough to worry about. "What's happening there?"

"Drambetsky's experts went through Madame Kwan's little black book," Zack exclaimed. "It's dynamite! Lists of telephone numbers, addresses and contact people at her 'warehouses' around the world where she 'stores' her immigrants. And we see VOCRA's place in her schemes, thanks to Luigi. I'll give you the details later. Madame Kwan doesn't know it yet, but she's finished and her worldwide operation is about to be shut down. You played a big part in all of this, Lilli. The FBI agents are singing your praises. Drambetsky's coming around to their way of thinking."

"Thank them for me," Lilli said, grateful that Zack and the agents were unharmed.

"You're sure you're okay after that scuffle with Madame Kwan's hellcats?"

"A hot bath soothed my aching muscles. I'm revved up and ready for whatever happens next."

"Dancing with me, I hope," Zack said. "I should be done here and back at Kate's by ten o'clock. Maybe we could go for a drink or a late supper? Someplace quiet where no one will recognize us."

"Sounds wonderful," Lilli said, but the uneasiness in his voice worried her. "Sure, I'll put John on. See you soon."

John took the phone from Lilli. "Right…right…no word on Bulldog, but…sure…I'll keep my eyes open," he promised Zack. "Don't worry. All the security lights are on and Officer Grady is guarding the front door. He's new and eager to make a name for himself. No one will get past him without a good fight. If they do—" John tapped his shoulder holster. "I'm ready."

"Lilli, how about a video?" Kate asked when John hung up. "I rented *Rear Window*."

"Great," Lilli said, stretching out on the living room couch. "I love Hitchcock and the film will take our minds off what's going on here." She tried to match Kate's forced cheerfulness.

"I'll be out of your way in a minute," John said, passing in front of the TV. Now that it was dark, he was rechecking all the windows and doors to make sure everything was locked tight. "I'll signal Officer Grady that everything is secure." He rapped his knuckles—three times and then once and then three times again—against the glass blocks in the panels flanking the door. A dark form moved across the glass blocks and Lilli knew that Officer Grady was on the job. The signal—three, one, three raps—came back loud and clear.

"Just like in a spy movie," Lilli said.

"For security purpose, it's best not to open the door," John said sternly. "And we can't count on the phones being secure. So, we use the old-fashioned method of tapping a code on the window. Sometimes, old-fashioned is the best way."

"I agree," Kate said, gazing at John. "Give me old-fashioned romance, an old-fashioned guy, and I'm hooked."

John didn't respond to Kate's comment about their budding romance. He was too busy checking the fuse box in the utility closet. He pulled four flashlights from his bag of supplies, tested them and set them on the kitchen counter. Apprehension gripped Lilli as darkness invaded The Trails.

"Lilli, how about helping me make some popcorn?" Kate asked.

Glad to keep busy, Lilli agreed.

"I'll be right back," John said, stepping past Kate's wheelchair. "I want to check out back by your studio. Probably just some alley cats looking for a handout, but I swear I heard something when I checked that window."

A slight tremor ran through Lilli as John headed to Kate's studio. Following Kate to the kitchen, Lilli glanced at the glass block panels by the front door and saw the dark form. Officer Grady was guarding the door.

Kate set the bag of popcorn in the microwave and pressed the timer for three minutes. Soon, the popcorn was popping noisily and Lilli set out a bowl and napkins. When the microwave timer rang, Lilli and Kate nearly jumped out of their skin. "Sorry," they both said and laughed nervously. Kate sprinkled the hot popcorn with salt and Lilli drizzled on melted butter.

"John's been gone an awfully long time," Kate said. She set the popcorn bowl on the coffee table.

Lilli slid the tape into the VCR and handed Kate the remote. "Stay here," she advised. "I'll find out what happened to him."

"I'll go with you," Kate said. "Something must be wrong."

An anxious feeling came over Lilli as she looked through the rear windows of Kate's studio. She didn't see John anywhere. Security lights cast eerie shadows in the flowers and shrubbery. The hanging baskets of spider plants looked like giant heads with scraggly hair bobbing and swaying in the stiff breeze. Their metal-chain hangers creaked and Lilli stifled a scream. She didn't see John. He must be out of her line of vision. "I don't like this," Lilli said. "I'll ask Officer Grady to see what's taking John so long. Wait here and promise me you won't open the door."

"But John could be hurt."

"John would want you to stay inside where it's safe."

Lilli rushed to the front door. She rapped out the code on the glass window: three, one, three.

No response. She rushed back to Kate's studio. Kate's face was drained of color. "Lilli," she said, her voice trembling, "I heard noises, like men's muffled voices, and then groans."

Lilli's hair prickled on the back of her neck. She gently pulled aside the slat of the vertical blind on the side window. John! John was lying on the ground near the flowerbeds. Bulldog was pulling himself up to his knees. He was dazed, shaking his head and moaning. Lilli saw the telephone wire dangling from the side of the house. Cut!

"Kate, don't speak above a whisper," Lilli insisted. "We need to telephone for help. Bulldog attacked John and Officer Grady."

"Are they alive?"

"I don't know." Lilli turned Kate's wheelchair toward the living room. "The phone wires are cut. Quick! Where's your cell phone?"

Kate gasped. "Zack borrowed it. It's upstairs in his room."

Hurrying to the foyer, Lilli saw a shadow through the glass blocks. It was much larger than before. It wasn't Officer Grady. Someone else was there.

Wind chimes tinkled in Kate's studio.

"Someone opened the back door," Kate said, her eyes wide with fear.

"Bulldog." Lilli's voice wavered. Both escape routes—the front and back doors—were now cut off. "The elevator," Lilli whispered. "We'll go to Zack's bedroom, lock ourselves in and phone the police for help."

As Lilli and Kate rode the elevator, they heard heavy footsteps stomp through the living room. Lamps crashed to the floor. Chairs and tables careened into the walls. Kate was steering herself out of the elevator behind Lilli as Bulldog charged up the stairs. He glared at Lilli, who was backed into the railing overlooking the foyer between the stairs and the elevator. "You nosy good-for-nothing redhead!" he bellowed, shaking his fist at her.

Kate headed toward the bedroom in a desperate attempt to reach her cell phone.

"Stay where you are," Bulldog shouted.

Ignoring him, Kate steered herself down the hallway.

Bulldog growled and raced after Kate. He grabbed the back of her wheelchair and spun it around, sending it back toward the staircase. Lilli dropped to her knees to stop the wheelchair from flying down the stairs, but Kate had propelled herself into the hallway wall. She blocked herself with her hands just as if she were charging into the tennis court fence.

"You gutless creep," Lilli cried. She began shadow boxing, jabbing with her fists, bouncing on her toes, imitating the martial arts moves from movies and TV. "Come and get me, dog-face," she snarled, edging away from the stairs. She raised one foot as if preparing to flip around and attack Bulldog with a high-flying kick.

Bulldog sneered. "I'll wipe the floors with you!"

"Try it," Lilli said fiercely, backing up against the railing.

"Redheads!" Bulldog bellowed. "You think you're so hot? Ha! I'll snuff you out like a cigarette butt!"

Out of the corner of her eye, Lilli saw Kate pick up two reams of computer paper. Kate hauled off and threw one at Bulldog. It nicked him in the shoulder. The second ream caught him full force behind the knees. His eyes bulged in startled surprise. He stumbled and fell toward Lilli. She grabbed the ream of paper and whacked him over the head.

Bulldog dragged himself to his feet. Enraged, bellowing like a wounded bull, he lumbered forward and grabbed at Lilli's throat. She reared back and ducked to the side. He flew over the railing.

THWAAACK! His massive body landed on the tiles below.

Lilli and Kate gripped the railing and looked down. Bulldog was sprawled on his stomach, lying on the bird design, motionless. His face was turned to the side. Blood trickled across the tiles like red fingers.

"I'll call the police," Kate said.

"Ssshhhh." Lilli touched Kate's arm. "Someone's in the living room." She heard the footsteps come toward the foyer. She and Kate backed away.

"Bulldog? Bulldog, ole buddy, you okay?" a man's gruff voice called out.

Next came a string of cuss words uttered in a raspy voice by another man. "Bulldog fell from up there," the raspy voice said.

"Is he dead?" the other man asked.

"Can't tell. Let's move him over to the couch."

"Come on," Lilli whispered to Kate, pointing at the bookcases. "We have to hide." She heard the grunts of the men downstairs as they dragged Bulldog from the foyer to the living room. She ran to Zack's room and grabbed the cell phone as Kate rolled herself toward the bookcases. Lilli rushed to her side and pushed the lever to open the storage room behind the bookcase. "Hurry," she whispered.

The bookcase moved silently.

Kate pushed hard but her wheelchair wouldn't go over the threshold track. "Save yourself," she whispered.

"We're in this together," Lilli whispered back. She

pushed the wheelchair hard, but it wouldn't ride over the track. "Get out of the chair and get in the crawl space," Lilli pleaded.

"I can't."

"Yes you can."

Fighting back tears, Kate lowered herself to the floor and dragged herself over the metal track and into the secret room.

"What's that noise upstairs?" the gruff voice growled.

Lilli rolled the wheelchair away from the computer into the corner next to the potted plant and fishing nets. She sneaked in behind Kate, turned around in the cramped quarters and faced the bookcase.

Footsteps rushed up the stairs.

Lilli tugged at the bookcase. It wouldn't budge. Please, please, she prayed and tugged harder. The footsteps were near the top of the stairs.

Swooooosh. The bookcase slid into place.

Kate reached forward and gripped Lilli's hand. They held on tightly, like drowning people grasping a life preserver. Lilli hoped the jackhammer pounding of their hearts couldn't be heard. She didn't dare use the cell phone. The intruder might hear her.

Lilli blinked, trying to accustom herself to the darkness. A sliver of light lined the side edges of the bookcase. A wedge of light spilled from above the top shelf. Lilli let go of Kate's hand, raised herself up and peered into the room. Slime and Greaser!

"Where did the broads go?" Slime said. "Redheads are always big trouble."

"And the babe in the wheelchair." Greaser kicked over the coffee table. "Where in blazes could she have gone? Her chair's right here and it's still warm."

Slime threw the potted plant. Greaser flung handfuls of magazines into the wall. He kicked the fishnets and tripped, cursing the fish and the net maker. Greaser stomped toward the bedrooms, trashing lamps and knickknacks. Slime remained where he was, inches from Lilli's eyes. He flailed around, tossing computer disks, reams of paper and books.

Greaser returned and kicked the wheelchair into the corner. "The babe's wheelchair has me spooked."

"Me, too," Slime said. "Let's get out of here."

Lilli grabbed the cell phone and was ready to punch in 911 when the front door slammed open.

"It's Madame Kwan's bodyguards," Slime said. Fear clung to his every word. "I told you we shouldn't mess with them. They wanted this job. Madame Kwan said it was theirs. But no, you had to have it. They won't let us out of here alive."

For the next several minutes, Lilli saw flashes of legs, boots, arms, tattoos, bandanas, metal and silk. The men grunted and groaned as they were beaten. The women squealed with delight with every kick, punch and chop they landed. With so much noise, Lilli chanced using the phone. She punched in 911.

A sudden shriek from one of the bodyguards frightened Lilli. The phone flew from her hands and slid along the floor. She heard it crash into the wall. Then there was a muffled sound and Lilli knew the phone had fallen into the insulation or an air conditioning duct. She and Kate groped around, but they couldn't find the phone. Panic overwhelmed Lilli. Their last chance for help was gone.

"The roof," Slime gasped, ducking a karate chop to the neck.

"Let's go," Greaser gasped.

Seconds later, Lilli heard the windows in Zack's bedroom crash.

Kate gasped. "They jumped onto the roof of my studio! They'll ruin my paintings!"

Lilli clamped her hand over Kate's mouth. The room beyond turned deadly silent. Then the bodyguards whispered in Chinese and poked at the bookcase shelves. They had heard Kate. They were searching for her and Kate right now, just beyond the thin wall that separated them.

Lilli peeked through the crack above the top shelf. She watched in horror as the two bodyguards, their eyes glistening with fury, backed away. One lifted the wheelchair. The other grabbed the office chair. They raised them over their heads, ready to propel them at the bookcases. Lilli ducked down. She clamped Kate's mouth and her own and protected Kate with her body. If they cried out and gave away their hiding place, they'd never survive.

Police sirens wailed in the distance, coming closer. Lilli prayed that a neighbor had heard the noise and called 911. She heard the bodyguards' footsteps retreat down the staircase. Coming from the back of the house, she heard Zack and Lobo's voices, and then John's voice, weak and rasping, saying something about handcuffing Bulldog.

"Thank God," Kate said. "John's alive."

Lilli pushed back the bookcase and crawled out. "Zack...Lobo...John," she screamed over the railing. "Watch out! Kwan's bodyguards are down there!" She heard footsteps coming from Kate's studio toward the living room. Then she heard scuffling, but couldn't see what was happening.

"I'll take this little hellcat," Zack shouted.

"I'll take that one," Lobo cried.

The four of them came into view, kicking and slugging it out, moving closer to the foyer. Lobo switched to karate moves and was winning his battle. Zack was giving it his best, but he was clearly losing.

Zack and the hellcat were now battling it out in the foyer directly beneath Lilli.

Lilli lifted the fishnet high over her head. "Move away, Zack!" she hollered and slung down the fishing net. It landed on the bodyguard, knocking her to the floor, where she lay trapped, on top of the mosaic bird. Battling with the fishnet, she struggled to free herself, but Zack grabbed her arms, pinned her and handcuffed her. She looked like a big cat in the wild, hissing and scratching, kicking at the bird that had managed to fly away.

"Okay, Kate," Lilli said. "It's safe to come out now." She helped Kate into her wheelchair. They rode downstairs together in the elevator. John and Officer Grady, who were in the living room, looked up and smiled weakly. They were guarding Bulldog, who was moaning and holding his head.

"Are my paintings okay?" Kate asked Zack.

"Stay back," Zack said, blocking the doorway to Kate's studio with his arm.

Lilli and Kate caught a glimpse of Slime and Greaser trapped in the domed ceiling, their feet dangling above Kate's paintings.

"Don't move, Greaser. You either, Slime," Zack snarled. "You could be electrocuted!"

"Oh, what shocking news!" Lilli joked, hoping her voice was calm and steady, hiding the fear that still gripped her.

TWENTY-FOUR

Luigi's Cantina

LILLI SETTLED INTO THE BACK booth in Luigi's Cantina where flickering candlelight, checkered tablecloths and dark wood created a cozy atmosphere. After the harrowing experiences of the past several days, Lilli enjoyed just sitting and gazing into Zack's eyes. A calm, peaceful feeling came over her even though noise and confusion reigned. Luigi and Mrs. D'Amato were entertaining dozens of VOCRA restaurant owners. They had thrown together an impromptu party to celebrate the downfall of Madame Kwan.

VOCRA president, Monsieur Renard, stood and raised his wineglass. "Thank you, Luigi and Mrs. D'Amato, for hosting this party. Thank you, Zack Faraday and Lilli Masters, for stopping Madame Kwan before she took control of our livelihood…and our lives. And thank you, loyal restaurant owners of Volusia County, for your confidence in my ability to continue as president. As for Madame Kwan, if she were here I would say, 'Bon appétit! Enjoy your prison food!'" Cheers echoed around the room and he continued speaking about VOCRA's joys and benefits.

Lilli's mind filled with Zack's account of the VOCRA convention in the Grand Pavilion after Agent Drambetsky had sent her away. Vendors touted the virtues of their cookbooks and cooking gadgets. Luigi and ninety-nine other VOCRA chefs cooked their specialties, which visitors eagerly sampled. Mrs. D'Amato sang passionately of her Italian homeland, reducing Luigi, a first-generation American from Napoli, to tears. Overcome with guilt, he admitted that VOCRA restaurants were profiting from the enforced labor of illegal immigrants. Slime and Greaser had pressured Monsieur Renard to force all the restaurant owners in VOCRA to hire illegal immigrants as dishwashers and kitchen helpers. VOCRA owners, who didn't have the resources of chains, such as legal counsel, had knuckled under. Madame Kwan's little black book contained a virtual blueprint of her plan to take over Florida, one county at a time, starting with Volusia.

"I still have a few questions," Lilli said. "What on earth did Madame Kwan have on Monsieur Renard?"

"When Renard first opened his restaurant, he bribed a health inspector. He's a proud man. He was afraid that if all this came out now, he could be stripped of his title as VOCRA president. His Canadian relatives flew in for the convention, and he didn't want to be embarrassed in their eyes. So several weeks ago, he gave in."

Relaxed and happy, Zack clicked the rim of his wineglass against Lilli's. "This case started with Benjamin Voda and the possibility of illegal gun sales. But it was never about Voda and guns; it was always about Madame Kwan and the exploitation of illegal immigrants. We just didn't see it right away. The two dead men—Vic Spiranza in New York and Ronny Miller in Tomoka Park—turned us in the right direction. They were weak links in Madame Kwan's chain of command. When they couldn't get their people to cooperate and kick in their share of the money, she ordered them killed." Zack shook his head. "Nothing turned out as I thought it would."

"But it turned out well," Lilli said. "Madame Kwan has been arrested."

"And Drambetsky says the case against her will stick."

"Coming to Florida was a big mistake for Madame Kwan," Lilli said. "Southern hospitality has taken on a new meaning."

Zack laughed. "Like rats from a sinking ship, her people are deserting her. Slime, Greaser, Bulldog and the guys who delivered roses to the Up-Down league have agreed to talk to the FBI in hopes of reduced sentences. Madame Kwan's empire is collapsing all around her."

Lilli sipped her wine. "Everything at work turned out well for you, too. Your boss wants you back on the job. And you and Kate seem to have made peace about the past."

"There's plenty of good news coming out of this case," Zack said. "Lobo and John will surely receive recognition for their work. And it looks like Frank Culhane will be able to put his life back together."

Just then Mrs. D'Amato burst into song, belting out "That's Amore."

Zack smiled. "That's Amore. That's love. That's something I've been wanting to, uh, well, you know, sort of tell you."

"Go ahead," Lilli said eagerly, hoping to hear him blurt out, 'I love you.'

Zack pulled a piece of paper from his pocket. "I'm not good with words off the top of my head, so I wrote this out." He unfolded the paper, cleared his throat and read: "Lilli, of all the plants and flowers I've seen in Tomoka Park and Bud's Blooms and on the internet, the most fascinating of all is your namesake, the lily." He looked up. "Sounds kind of stupid now that I hear it out loud."

Zack got up and came around to her side of the table. "Here's what I'm trying to say." He took her in his arms and kissed her. His lips were warm and inviting, his kiss was thrilling and she was deliriously happy. He didn't say, 'I love you,' but Lilli figured the night was still young.

* * * * *

REQUEST YOUR FREE BOOKS!

2 FREE NOVELS
PLUS 2 FREE GIFTS!

WORLDWIDE LIBRARY®
MYSTERY ™
Your Partner in Crime

YES! Please send me 2 FREE novels from the Worldwide Library® series and my 2 FREE gifts (gifts are worth about $10). After receiving them, if I don't wish to receive any more books, I can return the shipping statement marked "cancel." If I don't cancel, I will receive 4 brand-new novels every month and be billed just $4.99 per book in the U.S. or $5.99 per book in Canada. That's a saving of at least 25% off the cover price. It's quite a bargain! Shipping and handling is just 50¢ per book in the U.S. and 75¢ per book in Canada.* I understand that accepting the 2 free books and gifts places me under no obligation to buy anything. I can always return a shipment and cancel at any time. Even if I never buy another book, the two free books and gifts are mine to keep forever.

414/424 WDN FDDT

Name   (PLEASE PRINT)

Address   Apt. #

City   State/Prov.   Zip/Postal Code

Signature (if under 18, a parent or guardian must sign)

Mail to the **Reader Service:**
IN U.S.A.: P.O. Box 1867, Buffalo, NY 14240-1867
IN CANADA: P.O. Box 609, Fort Erie, Ontario L2A 5X3

Not valid for current subscribers to the Worldwide Library series.

Want to try two free books from another line?
Call 1-800-873-8635 or visit www.ReaderService.com.

* Terms and prices subject to change without notice. Prices do not include applicable taxes. Sales tax applicable in N.Y. Canadian residents will be charged applicable taxes. Offer not valid in Quebec. This offer is limited to one order per household. All orders subject to credit approval. Credit or debit balances in a customer's account(s) may be offset by any other outstanding balance owed by or to the customer. Please allow 4 to 6 weeks for delivery. Offer available while quantities last.

Your Privacy—The Reader Service is committed to protecting your privacy. Our Privacy Policy is available online at www.ReaderService.com or upon request from the Reader Service.

We make a portion of our mailing list available to reputable third parties that offer products we believe may interest you. If you prefer that we not exchange your name with third parties, or if you wish to clarify or modify your communication preferences, please visit us at www.ReaderService.com/consumerschoice or write to us at Reader Service Preference Service, P.O. Box 9062, Buffalo, NY 14269. Include your complete name and address.

WWLI1